Peter Conway lives in Somerset. He is a prolific writer, his most recent novel being *Deserving Death*.

DEADLY OBSESSION

Professor Helen Vaughan was a top scientist in the field of DNA research, and still only in her middle thirties. But she's found slumped over her desk in her office at the City Hospital, bludgeoned to death by a severe blow to the side of her head. Acerbic and both feared and disliked by her colleagues, she had a colourful private life featuring sado-masochistic games — as the police were soon to discover. Investigation into that, her traumatic upbringing and hospital tensions begin to reveal the deadly obsession that led to her death and the person responsible for it . . .

Books by Peter Conway
Published by The House of Ulverscroft:

LOCKED IN
UNWILLINGLY TO SCHOOL
DESERVING DEATH

PETER CONWAY

DEADLY
OBSESSION

Complete and Unabridged

ULVERSCROFT
Leicester

First published in Great Britain in 2008 by
Robert Hale Limited
London

First Large Print Edition
published 2008
by arrangement with
Robert Hale Limited
London

British Library CIP Data

Conway, Peter, *1929 –*
   Deadly obsession.—Large print ed.—
   Ulverscroft large print series: crime
   1. Detective and mystery stories
   2. Large type books
   I. Title
   823.9'14 [F]

   ISBN 978–1–84782–477–6

Published by
F. A. Thorpe (Publishing)
Anstey, Leicestershire

Set by Words & Graphics Ltd.
Anstey, Leicestershire
Printed and bound in Great Britain by
T. J. International Ltd., Padstow, Cornwall

This book is printed on acid-free paper

1

'Come in!'

'I've finished typing these minutes, Professor,' the diffident-looking woman said, looking down at the single sheet of paper in her hand. 'I thought you might like to check them one last time before I print the copies.'

The dark-haired, short, stockily built woman got up from the armchair, held out her hand and, without speaking, carefully read the contents.

'Yes, that makes everything clear. Would you take it down to Colonel Forbes and if he's happy with them, too, then perhaps you'd make copies and distribute them to all the other flats?'

'Very well, Professor.'

The woman came back fifteen minutes later to report that the colonel was quite happy with the document and that she had delivered the copies as requested.

'Thank you, Mrs Crawford.'

The prolonged ring on the front doorbell, followed by a series of violent thumps some ten minutes later, was not entirely unexpected and Helen Vaughan got to her feet as she heard the angry voice from the hall.

'Where is she?'

'Really, Mr Cahill — '

'It's all right, Mrs Crawford. Robert, come in here and sit down.' She made a gesture towards the half-open door of the sitting room, turned her back on him and went in herself. The man stared after her, for a moment seemed about to say something, then followed, his face flushed and the sheet of paper held so tightly that the knuckles of his right hand were showing white, and with obvious reluctance sat in the deep armchair.

'What the hell do you mean by this?' he said, lifting up the piece of paper.

'I would have thought it perfectly obvious. After all, you were at the extraordinary general meeting last Sunday when it was agreed that the next half-yearly maintenance charge should be doubled in order to pay for the re-roofing of the garages.'

'I never agreed to that, as you bloody well know; the estimates for the work are far too high and I, for one, have no intention of paying.'

'I take it you haven't lost your copy of the Articles of Association of our company. If you have, or haven't read them recently, let me remind you. Decisions are taken by a majority of leaseholders at meetings at which there must be a quorum of at least six members and are binding. At our last meeting, seven of us were present as indicated in the minutes, of which you have just received a copy, and the decision about the maintenance charge was carried by a majority of five to one, with the chairman not voting. Your objections were also recorded and the chairman is happy with the minutes. Should you fail to pay your contribution within a reasonable period of time, the details of which will be sent out within the next few days, the matter will be put in the hands of the company's solicitors. I trust I make myself clear.'

The man, purple in the face, screwed up the piece of paper. 'That's what I think of your fucking minutes and — '

'And what, Robert?'

'You'll soon see.'

'I don't take kindly to threats, Robert, and suggest you calm down, think matters out carefully and I look forward to receiving the cheque for your maintenance charge within two weeks of your receiving the formal notification.'

Cahill, his face livid, got up, his fists clenched, and then stormed out of the room, slamming both living room and front doors behind him.

Helen Vaughan went out into the corridor and beckoned to the woman who was hovering at the end of the corridor.

'After that little exhibition, I think a cup of coffee and chocolate biscuit are called for, Mrs Crawford: I also feel in need of some fresh air, so perhaps you would bring it out to me on the balcony.'

She was sipping her coffee, once again admiring the view across the golf course towards the spire of St Mary's church, when she heard the roar of the engine of the 4×4, the cracked silencer adding to the noise, and as she stood up to look over the balustrade, she saw Cahill's car, tyres squealing, as it lurched on to the road, canting over on its springs. It had just begun to straighten up when there came the squeal of locked wheels, a loud bang and the tinkle of shattered glass falling on to the tarmac. Within seconds, Cahill was out on the road, screaming abuse at the driver of the car that had run into the back of him, before getting back into his own vehicle, which bucketed down the hill and out of sight.

Pausing only to pick up her mobile phone, Helen Vaughan hurtled down the five flights of stairs, taking them two at a time, then ran across the forecourt out on to the road. A young woman was standing in front of her

4

car, ashen white and trembling as she looked at the shattered headlights and the front of the Nissan Micra, which was buckled with an ominous trickle of water coming from the fractured radiator.

Helen Vaughan put her arm round the woman's shoulders. 'What's your name?'

'Christine.'

'Mine's Helen. Why not sit on the wall there for a moment? Don't worry, I saw what happened and it wasn't your fault at all. I've got the number of that 4×4 and I'm going to send for the police. You're not hurt, are you?' The woman shook her head. 'That's the most important thing. You've had a nasty shock, though. How about a mug of tea? Do you take sugar?' There was another nod. 'What about a warning triangle?'

'I don't have one.'

Her voice was only just audible and she began to shiver.

'I've got one in the garage and I'll fetch it in a minute or two. I promise that you won't be left on your own; either my secretary or I will stay with you until all this has been dealt with.'

When the young woman nodded, Helen led her across to the low wall, sat down beside her and tapped out the number of her flat on her mobile phone.

'Mrs Crawford, there's been an accident in the road outside and the young lady I'm with is uninjured, but badly shocked. I'd like you to bring down a mug of tea, sugar and some tissues. I'm going to ring the local police — the number will be in the local phone book — and perhaps you'd bring that down with you as well as my car keys and the gadget for opening the garage. They're both on the shelf above the radiator in the hall.'

Helen Vaughan had had previous dealings with the local police over a break-in through the rear door of the block and when she got through to them and mentioned the name of the sergeant who had come round on that occasion, they promised to send a car over. After she had placed the warning triangle from her garage some twenty yards above the damaged vehicle, she went back to the young woman. Some of her colour had come back, but tears were still trickling down her cheeks.

Helen wiped them away and gave her a hug. 'Cheer up. I'm quite prepared to act as a witness for you.'

'But I'm only insured for third party and I . . .'

'I'll help you to sort all that out later.'

* * *

Christine Prior was never to forget that morning — it was as if she had been carried along by an irresistible force. To start with, there had been Helen Vaughan's reassurance and comforting words and then her advice about how to handle the police.

'It's important that you stick to a straightforward account of what happened,' she had said. 'Don't embellish it, but don't leave anything out and be sure to tell them exactly what that man said to you. Don't be embarrassed and use his exact words. From where I was, I couldn't make them out, but I'm quite sure you remember them. Let's go over what you're going to say to them now and you'll find it much easier the second time round.'

It helped that her driving licence and insurance certificate were in her handbag and the two police officers, a man and a woman, were polite and considerate. A breakdown firm took the car away and that was by no means the end of it. Helen Vaughan gave her a cold lunch, advised her to ring her insurance company straightaway and then gave her the name of a solicitor, assuring her that she would give evidence if the incident came to court. Finally, she drove her back to her flat in Balham.

'Why do you suppose that woman went to

all that trouble to help you?' her boyfriend Rob said when Christine told him what had happened. 'Did she fancy you, or something?'

It felt as if an ice cube had been dropped down the back of her neck, but somehow she managed to shake her head and retain her presence of mind.

'Don't be ridiculous,' she said, feeling herself flushing and hoping against hope that he would interpret it as anger. 'I've been really shaken up and I'm not in the mood for remarks like that. If you must know, that woman was really nice and told me that she knew the man who had caused the crash, that he was a bully, that it was all his fault, that she wasn't going to let him get away with it and would be happy to act for me as a witness.'

She breathed a sigh of relief when he apologized and gave her a hug, but she wasn't going to tell Rob, or anyone else, for that matter, what had really happened when she had gone into her flat with Helen. She had winced slightly, when she was taking off her coat, and the woman had noticed it at once.

'Did the steering wheel catch you?'

'No, my chest's just been a bit sore since I went forward against the seatbelt.'

'You'd better let me take a look at it — I'm a doctor, you know.' She made a soft clicking noise with her tongue when she saw the reddened and rough area on the side and front of her right breast. 'No wonder it's sore. Got any cream I could rub in?'

'There's some Savlon in the bathroom.'

'That'll do nicely.'

The feeling, when the woman had put some of the cream on her forefinger and began a gentle circular movement over the affected area, was indescribable, quite different from anything Rob had ever done to her. He was always too rough and never seemed to find exactly the right spot, but this time it felt as if she was melting, and then her nipple came to attention and she let out a gasp.

'Do you want me to stop?'

Later, she was to remember and never forget what followed. Too embarrassed to say anything, she shook her head and the astonishing feelings that had followed and went right to the very centre of her as the knowing fingers and tongue began to explore the rest of her, doing things she had read about but never experienced before, drove her to a crescendo of previously never experienced pleasure. She told herself later that her reactions had merely been the result of the shock following the car crash, but she knew that that wasn't true and that she had discovered things about herself that were going to be very difficult to come to terms with.

2

On the occasions that Superintendent Roger Tyrrell went into the Yard early, he enjoyed the drive. At that time of the morning, there was little traffic about and King's Road was looking its best with the roses out in many of the gardens. He arrived in his office just before seven and immediately started work on the files that had been piling up over the previous week. He had been hard at it for nearly an hour when the phone rang.

'Tyrrell.'

'It's Brandon here. I've just had Sir David Buxton on the line. He's the chairman of the board of the City Hospital. Evidently one of their star pathologists, a woman called Helen Vaughan, has been found dead in her office this morning by her secretary and she gave the chief executive a ring, who immediately contacted Buxton for advice. The woman sounds to be a pretty cool customer; most people would have dialled 999 at once, that is, if they had been in a fit state to do so. Thank the Lord I found you in — this is going to need handling with great care. What do you suggest?'

'I'll mobilize my team, Inspectors Prescott and Sinclair, a couple of excellent people, get over there myself as soon as possible and I'll also give the forensic pathologist a ring. There's no way we're going to keep this quiet, sir, and I won't be able to manage the media on top of everything else.'

'You've no need to worry about that — I'll deal with them.'

'How will I contact the secretary woman when I get there?'

'Give her a ring first. Her name's Enid Ashby and she's going to wait in her office until we get in touch with her — I'll give you her extension number.'

Tyrrell sat there for a moment after the commissioner had rung off. He knew about Helen Vaughan, having attended a lecture she gave to senior members of the CID on the latest trends in DNA technology, and also knew what a sensation this was going to cause.

Having made his calls, Tyrrell drove to the hospital and, as he had arranged on the phone, met Miss Ashby in the front hall. She was a tall, thin woman, probably, he thought, in her early fifties, wearing thick glasses and dressed in a brown skirt and matching blouse. There was no hint of stress in her expression, her hand was dry when she shook his and she spoke in a precise, clipped fashion.

'I'll take you up to the department straightaway,' she said when she had introduced herself. 'The door to the main entrance has a keypad entry system, which is why I thought it best if I came down here to meet you.'

Neither of them spoke as they went up in the lift and she entered the code on the pad beside the double doors, above which was a large plastic strip with the words 'PATHOLOGY DEPARTMENT' in large letters on it.

'Professor Vaughan's office is at the end of this corridor here.'

'I gather that its door was unlocked when you arrived here this morning.'

'Yes and that is the first time I can ever remember it being so at that time of day. I come in every weekday morning just before 7.30 in order to let the cleaner in and stay with her until she has finished. You see, the professor was always most insistent that any papers on her desk should not be disturbed and so I always looked after the dusting on her desk myself.'

Tyrrell noted with interest the use of the past tense and nodded. 'Who else apart from you and Professor Vaughan had keys to her office?'

12

'No one.'

'Why was security so tight?'

'The professor had a worry, almost amounting to paranoia, that someone might gain access to this laboratory and have a sight of her results prior to publication.'

'Did she often come into work at weekends?'

'Only when she had an important paper or lecture to prepare and provided she didn't require the use of the library.'

'Where did she live?'

'In a flat in Wimbledon.'

'Alone?'

'No, she had a resident housekeeper.'

'She wasn't married, then?'

'No.'

It was scarcely detectable, but there had been a subtle change in the woman's expression as she said it; it was nothing more than a slight narrowing of her eyelids, but he was quite sure of it.

'Did she come in to work by car?'

'She did at the weekends, but usually preferred the underground on weekdays.'

Tyrrell had already decided to wait until his team and the forensic people had arrived before taking any further action and noted that the woman did not appear in the least curious or disturbed by that, either before or after he had explained why he thought it necessary.

'So you see, I want the experts in this part of our work to have as undisturbed a field as possible. Do you remember if you touched anything when you went in to the room?'

'Inevitably I had to use the door handle when entering, but as soon as I was inside and saw that the professor was dead, I was extremely careful not to touch anything else.'

'Would you tell me exactly what you saw, please?'

The woman didn't hesitate. 'The ceiling strip lights were on as was the small lamp on the desk and the professor was slumped forward over it, with the right side of her head resting on some papers. It looked as if the left side of her head had received a severe blow; there was clotted blood there and the bone had obviously been crushed. Her eyes were open and it was clear to me that she was dead. I couldn't fail to notice, either, that her paperweight was missing. It was a glass one with an intricate pattern of flowers in it and roughly hemispherical in shape with a green beige cloth stuck to its base. I remember remarking once to the professor how beautiful it was and she told me that it was associated with very special memories for her.'

'Are you quite sure that it was there earlier in the week?'

'Oh yes. As usual, I dusted the desk on Friday morning and it was quite definitely there then.'

'Can you give me some idea of how big that paperweight was?'

The woman hesitated for a moment. 'Rather more than half a large grapefruit, I would say. I remember that the base filled my hand when I picked it up to examine it carefully when the professor showed it to me and before I did so, she warned me to be very careful as it was so heavy and indeed it was.'

'When did you start to work for Professor Vaughan?'

'I came with her from St Gregory's when she was appointed as reader here five years ago — she was a senior lecturer there. She was given a personal chair the year before last.'

'Was she popular here?'

'The professor had a habit of being right about most things; she was also very direct and some people found both those things unsettling.'

'I see. Did you like her personally yourself?'

'I have worked with academics for the best part of twenty years, Superintendent, and I have never let personal feelings enter into my relationships with them.'

My God, Tyrrell thought, she's a cold fish. She had been with Professor Vaughan for many years, had obviously been trusted by her — the fact that she had been allowed to hold the only spare key to the office made that clear — and yet, here she was, a mere forty minutes or so after she had found the woman dead in horrible circumstances, and hadn't turned a hair.

'Perhaps you'd be good enough to let me have your key. I presume that the other one is — '

At that moment, there was a loud knock on the door at the main entrance to the department and a few minutes later, the corridor was filled by men and women in protective gear.

'The scene-of-crime people are bound to take some time,' Tyrrell said to his two assistants who had arrived a few minutes after them, 'but I think it would be a good idea for us all to hear what Tredgold has to offer before I speak to the commissioner about a press release and make my number with the chief executive and the senior members of the department here. After that, I'd like you both to go down to Wimbledon and take a look at the professor's flat. Miss Ashby will be able to give you the address and phone number. I

16

gather that there's a resident housekeeper, but I'll leave it to you to decide whether or not to give her a ring first.'

The forensic pathologist arrived some twenty minutes later and when he emerged from the office half an hour after that, almost for the first time that Tyrrell could remember, the man had a serious expression on his face. 'Bad business, this,' he said in his rasping voice.

'Professor Vaughan was working in your field of research, wasn't she, Eric?'

'Yes, if you can call the application of other people's work, research, which in all justice I don't think one can; the difference between her and me could be likened to that between a Ferrari and a Trabant.'

'Did you know her personally?'

'Not really, and offhand I can't think of anyone working in pathology who did. Personal popularity most certainly wasn't on her agenda. Enough of the cod psychology; she had been on the receiving end of a single, severe blow to the left side of the head, which produced a depressed fracture of the temporal bone.'

'Her secretary told me that a large and very heavy glass hemispherical paperweight, which had certainly been on her desk last Friday, was missing; do you think that something like that might have been the weapon?'

'It's a possibility.'

'If that was the case, the murderer must have been a very cool customer indeed, presumably not wearing gloves and realizing immediately that incriminating fingerprints or DNA would have been left behind.'

Tredgold gave one of his vulpine smiles. 'Your logic, my dear Tyrrell is, as always, impeccable, but aren't you doing a little gun jumping? Perhaps it would be prudent to discuss the matter further when I have finished the autopsy and, in the meantime, before you ask, the time of death is very difficult to determine — one window was slightly open and it was quite warm last night. However, I would say it was roughly twelve hours ago, but not much longer than that. Come to see me when I've done the full autopsy. Give Miss Tombs a ring first thing tomorrow morning; if you're in luck, that troglodyte of a woman might have emerged from her cave and be able to give you an appointment.'

Tyrrell waited until the man had departed and then turned towards his assistants.

'You know the man of old, Sarah, but what did you make of him, Mark?'

'He reminds me very much of Rawlings, the forensic pathologist with whom I worked a couple of times when I was with Thames Valley. His saving grace was that beneath the veneer of an acerbic misogynist, he was, in fact, quite a sympathetic character and I liked him.'

Tyrrell smiled. 'I will be interested to see if you warm to our friend Tredgold as well. Right, I'll have a word with Pocock before we leave and see if I can prise the keys of the flat from him. The housekeeper will obviously have those for the front door of the block and the flat, but you never know, there may be a safe, or something like that.'

The head of the scene-of-crime team answered Tyrrell's knock on the door of the laboratory himself and after a minute or two's discussion, the detective came back with a bunch of keys.

'These were found in the pocket of the professor's sheepskin jacket, which was hanging on a hook behind the door. Pocock's kept some of them, the one to this door, those of the filing cabinets and that of her car, which may well be in the consultants' car park. I gather she often comes in it if she is working at the weekend, and he's going to take a look at it later. I'm just going to have a word with McKenzie, the head of the department, and his senior colleagues, and I'd like you to give me a ring on my mobile later on to let me know how you've got on. All right?'

★ ★ ★

Alastair McKenzie was a powerfully built man with thick grey hair and, Tyrrell thought, looked to have been in his late fifties. He had a soft lowland Scottish accent and seemed quite at ease as he sat behind his desk, his hands resting on the top of it.

'This must have come as a terrible shock to you,' the detective said.

'It has.'

'Perhaps you would tell me about Professor Vaughan, particularly any personal details. I already know something about her research interests from Dr Tredgold, whom you no doubt know — I imagine you are familiar with most of the people in London working in your field.'

'Yes, I know Tredgold.'

McKenzie sounded distinctly less than enthusiastic, but knowing of old the forensic pathologist's spiky and acerbic personality, Tyrrell was not in the least surprised.

'Helen Vaughan was, I would say, well on the way to becoming the most distinguished and talented research worker we have ever had, not only in our department, but in the hospital and medical school as a whole. She was, though, not an easy person to have as a colleague. The expression 'not suffering fools gladly' might have been invented to describe her. It is one thing to disagree with people, but quite another to put them down with ill-disguised scorn and the fact that she was almost always right didn't make it any easier, either. She also rowed on the crest of the wave of female superiority, which has become so fashionable, not that she was so lacking in subtlety that she ever expressed it quite like that. If a man is being arrogant and overbearing, it is easy enough to tell him so directly and forcibly, but most males still hesitate to do the same to a woman, particularly if he is one of my generation.'

'Did anyone here feel so strongly about her that they might even have wanted to kill her?'

'The very idea is absurd. In this department, we all respected her greatly, but there were several who didn't like her as a person.'

'Were you one of them?'

'One of the necessary attributes of a successful head of a hospital department, even a relatively small one like this, is not to let personal likes and dislikes get in the way of the cohesion and smooth-running of the various sections. I like to think that I have always borne that in mind and that I have succeeded in so doing.'

'What about her personal life outside her work?'

'That was a closed book as far as I was concerned and I venture to suggest that that was also true of all my colleagues.'

'Do any of your staff ever come in to work on Sunday evenings?'

'Yes. There are technicians and consultants on call in all the sections. Occasionally, emergency blood grouping, chemical analyzes and examination of pathological specimens are required — it doesn't happen all that often.'

'What about yesterday?'

'Everyone has to sign in; some years ago fiddling of expenses for on-call duties was going on here, which was why that measure was introduced, and the only record yesterday was of some electrolyte analyzes being required in the morning.'

'But presumably anyone knowing the code to the door of the main entrance to your department could just have walked in.'

'That is true.'

'Were you on call yourself yesterday?'

'Yes, I was.'

'Would you be good enough to tell me what you were doing that evening, Professor? Let me assure you that that is a question I will be asking a great many people,' Tyrrell said with a smile.

The man nodded, his serious expression not changing. 'I went to visit my wife, as I do every Sunday, carrying my pager as is my habit whenever I am on call. She is and has been in a nursing home for more than twenty years now; ever since she had a catastrophic asthma attack, which left her severely brain damaged due to lack of oxygen. After that, I returned to my flat to read and listen to some music.'

'I'm very sorry, I didn't know about your wife and I'm very concerned to hear of it. I'm sure you'd like to be kept informed about our progress and I will get in touch with you again later.'

Tyrrell's conversations with the other senior members of the department amounted to little more than making introductions, apart that is from Spencer, McKenzie's number two in the section of morbid anatomy. There was something about him that attracted Tyrrell's attention, a trace of excitement perhaps, an anxiety to please, and the detective made a mental note to get his team to follow that up.

3

'Do you think we should ring the house-keeper now?' Sinclair asked Sarah when they were in the corridor outside Miss Ashby's office, after having obtained the address and phone number of Professor Vaughan's flat from her.

'I'm against it,' Sarah said. 'I'd like to see her reaction face to face when we break the news.'

'I agree.'

The block of flats was very close to the All England Tennis Club and Sarah parked the car in the forecourt. They let themselves in with one of the keys on the bunch and went into the lift in the lobby and up to the top floor. In response to their ring, the door was opened on a chain by a rather faded-looking woman of medium build, with brown hair with flecks of grey in it, who looked to be in her late forties or early fifties.

'Yes?'

'Police,' Sarah said, holding out her warrant card. 'We've come about Professor Vaughan.'

'Is anything wrong?' the woman asked after

she had let them in.

'You are?'

'I'm the professor's housekeeper — Mrs Crawford.'

'There's no way of putting this gently, I'm afraid. The professor is dead — she's been murdered.'

The woman sat down heavily on the chair by the telephone. 'I was speaking to her at the hospital on the phone only yesterday evening.'

'Weren't you worried when she wasn't here for breakfast this morning?'

'No. You see, she sometimes stayed at the hospital overnight if she had been working very late. There are a number of guest rooms that are normally used for patients' relatives and staff are allowed to use them if there are any vacancies. She was also able to get breakfast there as well.'

'What time was the phone call?'

'She left here at about five o'clock yesterday afternoon to work on her new book and she rang me soon after seven. She wanted me to read out a list of references that she had failed to take with her. Originally, I was trained as a secretary and used to do some work for her here on the word processor as well as acting as her housekeeper.'

'How long was the call?'

'Not more than two or three minutes.'

'And she sounded her usual self then?'

'Oh yes.'

'Did she often go up to the hospital at weekends?'

'Not until recently when she started to work on her new book.'

'What about leisure time?'

'She used to take some holiday after the many overseas conferences she attended and quite often had visitors here for the weekend when she liked me to move out. She organized for me to stay at a guesthouse in Putney on those occasions — she had an arrangement with the woman there who runs it so that there was always a room for me or the professor's visitors from abroad. The professor always gave me plenty of notice — she was punctilious about that sort of thing.' The woman bent forwards and passed her hand across her forehead.

'Would you like a drink of water?'

'No, thank you, I'll be all right in a moment.'

A few minutes later, when she had recovered her composure, the woman showed them round. The flat occupied the whole of the top floor of the block. Opposite the entrance was a double door which led into the very large L-shaped sitting room, and

26

there was access to a long balcony on the southwest side. They made their way along that and then through a similar door at the other end into the kitchen.

'This was originally a dining room,' the housekeeper said, as they went into the last room on that side of the flat, 'but it's now my sitting room.'

The two detectives looked briefly at the sofa, the large armchair and the TV in the corner and then at the woman's bedroom, which was of good size and with a view of the garden at the back.

'This was the double spare room originally and in here,' she said, opening the next door on the other side of the corridor, 'is the office.'

It was well equipped with a laptop, printer, photocopier and fax and next to it, there was another small single bedroom with a bath-room and lavatory in separate rooms along a short side passage.

'And what's round the corner along the corridor beyond the main sitting room?' Sarah asked.

'I don't know exactly.'

'I don't understand.'

The woman showed them the door, which was just out of sight and fitted with a combination entry pad.

'I've never been beyond this door.'

'Who does the cleaning in the flat?'

'I do the day-to-day tidying up and a woman comes once a week to do the heavier work, but she never goes in this room, either. The professor looked after it herself.'

'Did she ever explain the reason for that?'

'No, and I never asked. The professor wasn't the sort of person to encourage questions of that sort.'

'Does that staircase outside the front door lead to the flat roof?'

'Yes. There is also a large sun room up there, which the professor owned as well.'

'Are the other residents allowed up on the roof terrace?'

'No, apart from Colonel Forbes, who supervises the maintenance of the lift and the water tanks, which are both in a separate housing up there.'

'I don't suppose the rest of the residents are all that pleased about that.'

'Most of them accept it; after all, the other flats cost a great deal less than this one. The one big bone of contention has been the maintenance of the flat roof, the concrete surround and balustrade, all of which are maintained by the company, of which the flat owners are all directors as long as they hold leases. Some of them, though, think that the professor ought to be solely responsible for that part of the block and although they obviously had a point, she got a legal opinion on the leases and that came down firmly in her favour. After that, there was no further argument except from Mr Cahill, who has never accepted it.'

'Mr Cahill?'

'He is the owner of flat seven.'

Sinclair saw the flush spreading up the woman's cheeks and managed to catch Sarah's eye, almost imperceptibly shaking his head, then raised the bunch of keys in his hand.

'We'll just have a look up top,' he said, 'and then we'd like to have another word with you.'

The two of them climbed the staircase from the landing and Sinclair unlocked the door at the top.

'Sorry to interrupt like that but I couldn't make that woman's reaction out at all,' Sinclair said.

'How do you mean?'

'Well, I was watching her carefully when you broke the news about Helen Vaughan's murder and although she did seem shocked initially, she recovered remarkably quickly and the only real emotion she showed afterwards was when Cahill's name came up.

I thought that if we pressed her too hard, she might clam up altogether.'

Sarah nodded. 'Good point. There's bound to be someone here who knows everyone's business, perhaps the colonel, who, if he comes up here regularly, must have got on at least reasonably well with Helen Vaughan.' She looked round. 'What an absolutely stunning view!'

The flat roof was surrounded by a concrete wall about three feet high and on top of it was a substantial metal balustrade, which looked practically new. To the east they had a clear sight of Battersea Power Station, the London Eye, the Gherkin and, in the far distance, Canary Wharf, while to the south was a golf course, with a lake in the middle of it, and the All England Tennis Club dominated the view to the west.

'Quite staggering, the whole thing. I've never seen a flat to equal it.'

'Nor I.'

The sun room had a solid roof, but with large glass windows on three sides, all fitted with blinds, and there was a double bed with a cover and cushions strewn over it, a table and several wicker chairs and a large whiteboard on a stand.

'What do you think, Sarah?'

'I'm particularly intrigued by that door

with the combination entry pad on it and we need to get Jack Pocock down here as soon as possible to open it and deal with whatever there is behind it.'

'I agree. The whole door's obviously a recent addition and when I looked over the balustrade on the flat roof, I could see what were obviously the windows to a large room behind it and the frosted glass on the south side suggests another bathroom as well. We'd better give Tyrrell a ring first and then there's the question of the housekeeper. We really need her out of the way before we leave and Pocock gets here.'

That proved no problem as even though Mrs Crawford didn't have a key to the guesthouse, Mrs Haddon, the woman who ran it, said she would be there all morning when Sinclair phoned her. And, business being slack, Mrs Crawford would be able to stay there as long as necessary.

'We'd be grateful if you'd go there as soon as possible after you've had time to collect what you require for your stay,' Sinclair said to the housekeeper after he had rung off. 'Should you need anything else, please get in touch with me on my mobile and we'll make the necessary arrangements. I must ask you, though, not to leave London and remain based at the guesthouse for the time being as we may need to see you again. Oh, and one last thing: we'd like to talk to one of the other residents and we wondered if you would be able to recommend someone who knew the professor well.'

The woman didn't hesitate. 'Colonel Forbes would be the best person — he helped the professor with the administration of the block. He lives with his wife in flat eight and he should be back from his daily game of golf by now.'

'Will you be able to get to Putney all right?'

'Yes, thank you. I won't need a large case and the 39 bus goes almost from door to door.'

★   ★   ★

After the woman had gone, the two detectives walked down the stairs to the landing two floors below and rang the bell of flat eight. The man who opened the door was dressed in an open-necked shirt with a cravat and a fawn jumper, light green slacks and highly polished brown shoes.

'Police?' he said, raising one eyebrow. 'What's that tearaway of a wife of mine been up to now? Picking someone's flowers from their garden or perhaps nicking their favourite gnome, I shouldn't wonder.'

'What are you going on about now, Alec, you silly man? Aren't you going to ask them in?'

The woman who had come waddling down the passageway was as untidy as her husband was immaculate. The loose, off-white shift she was wearing would have passed as night attire, which, Sarah thought, it might well have been, her hair didn't look as if it had been acquainted with a brush for some considerable time and her ankles were overflowing the top of a pair of distinctly tired-looking bedroom slippers.

'Sorry, m'dear.' He turned towards the two detectives. 'Not long back from me daily round of golf, don't yer know? Fred Gaines and I are on the tee at 6.30 sharp every morning come rain come shine and back in the clubhouse by 8.45 for a quick shower, followed by a hearty breakfast. Nothing like it for setting one up for the rest of the day.'

No wonder, Sarah thought, as he ushered them into the living room, that the man's wife had long since decided that trying to compete with him in the hearty and clothing stakes was a complete waste of a time.

'Now, what can we do for you?'

They listened in silence as Sinclair told him what had happened to Helen Vaughan.

'What a terrible thing!' the colonel said, shaking his head.

'Did you know her well?'

'Not exactly well, but better than anyone else here, particularly after the court case.'

'Court case?'

'Yes. There's a fellow called Robert Cahill who lives with his wife across the landing from us and he disliked Helen right from the moment she came here five years ago. Following the accident, he hated her. It must have been about eighteen months ago, a Saturday as I recall, and the reason I know about it was that I attended the hearing at the local magistrates' court. I like to say that it was to see fair play, but Madge won't have that; she thinks the only reason I went was to see Cahill get his comeuppance and she may have a point.'

'What sort of accident was it?'

'Let me explain. It was a Saturday morning and Cahill had had a row over the minutes of a special meeting we had to consider having a one-off increase in the maintenance charge to cover the re-roofing of the garages, saying he had no intention of paying any extra despite the agreement of all the others attending. Of course, Helen, being Helen, gave as good as she got and told him that she would put the company's solicitor on to him unless he did so and he stormed out of the building and got into his car. It is one of those beastly 4×4 off-road things with bull bars back and front and makes a noise like a Zeppelin — at least, it did until he was forced to get the silencer repaired after the accident. Anyway, he shot out of the drive, leaving tyre marks as he skidded round on to the road, and a young woman who was coming down the hill wasn't able to stop in time and hit him from behind. He got out, screamed abuse at her and drove off, spinning his wheels.

'How do I know all this? Well, it all came out at the court case. Helen was on her balcony and saw the whole thing. She wasn't the sort of person to hang around in a situation like that. Down she went, comforted the woman, whose car was buckled in the front, rang the police and when they arrived, told them what she had seen, gave them the number of Cahill's car and said she was quite prepared to be a witness if the incident resulted in court action.'

'And it obviously did.'

'It most certainly did. Cahill had his solicitor with him, whose line was that Helen and Robert had never got on and perhaps that had coloured her recollection of events. If he hoped to get her to rise to that or lose her rag, he must have been sadly disappointed. She was unshakeable and when the solicitor suggested that her memory of events, which had occurred some months earlier, might have been faulty, she fixed the man with those startling blue eyes of hers and said that she had written a detailed letter about the incident to the Medical Defence Union that very afternoon and held up a copy of it. The chairman, or perhaps I should say chairperson, as she was a formidable, no-nonsense woman, one of the tweed skirt and sensible brogues brigade, after taking advice from the clerk, read the letter and asked Helen why she had done that. I remember very clearly what she said. 'Although I no longer practise clinical medicine, I am a fully qualified medical doctor and it is the advice of the Medical Defence Union that if one attends an accident, it is wise to inform them of the circumstances and what action you took. Although the young woman was unhurt apart from a minor friction burn from her seatbelt, I thought it prudent to follow their advice, hence the letter.'

'The gist of her evidence was that Cahill was in an agitated state when he left her flat, that he had driven out of the drive at speed and that the woman in the car coming down the hill had no chance of stopping in time. Helen made no attempt to embroider her evidence and remained icily calm throughout. There followed technical details from the police about the tyre marks on the road and the condition of the young woman's car, which had a current MOT certificate and was found to be in good order apart from the accident damage, which was considerable. White paint from the Nissan had been found on the rear bumper of Cahill's car and the pattern of the tyre marks on the road were consistent with his vehicle having turned out of the forecourt of the block at considerable speed.'

'And the upshot?'

'He was fined for careless driving and failing to stop and give his details after an accident. He already had points on his licence for a couple of earlier speeding offences and had it taken away for a year, despite special pleading that it would be impossible to do his job without it. The magistrate was totally unmoved by that and also took the opportunity to let him know that his behaviour at the time of the accident was unacceptable and that it would be in his interests to consider taking advice about anger management.'

'Not much love lost between him and

Helen Vaughan, then?'

'You could certainly say that and he never seemed to learn — they were always having rows at our management committee meetings and I remember that on one occasion he completely lost his rag and shouted at her, even threatening her.'

'In what way?'

'Just saying that one of these days she was going to get her comeuppance. When I was secretary of the maintenance company, I always favoured the tactful, careful approach to disagreements, but when she took over, she always waded in, all guns blazing. Helen could be painfully abrupt and direct, but I have never known anyone better organized or efficient and she was invariably well prepared. That was the thing that sank Cahill; he was always complaining about something, but never seemed to learn that to be effective one has to do one's homework and she always seemed to be able to put him down by producing some piece of evidence that he clearly had never thought of. Cahill is also a bully, but one look from those astonishing blue eyes of hers always seemed to emasculate him completely — in my view his blustering was just a tactic to avoid loss of face.'

'What did the others here think about her?'

'Well, there's no doubt that her methods put people's backs up and it must be said that this place is not as happy as it used to be. I'm not saying that that was entirely Helen's fault, but she did make some of the older people uncomfortable. However, there was never any shoddy workmanship in any of the projects that she supervised; she was only too ready to face up to anyone, but only when she had all the facts both buttoned up and at her fingertips.'

'Her flat at the top is so different from the others that we couldn't help wondering how it came about,' Sinclair said.

The colonel smiled. 'It was designed and lived in for a number of years by the man who owned and financed the building of this block — that's why it's so much better appointed and bigger than all the others. He owned the freehold of the block, too, and held on to it for a time after he left and a separate lease for the top flat was sold to Helen's predecessor, Arthur Bright. When the residents bought the freehold later, they tried to get access to the flat roof, but Arthur wouldn't have it and quite right, too. Cahill was never able to accept that and over the years kept niggling about it, never more so than when Helen bought it, but typically, she had armed herself with a legal opinion and there was nothing he could do about it.'

'Is Cahill about today?'

'Not at the moment. He will leave his car in the forecourt the whole time, although not only is that against one of the covenants in the lease, but, like everyone else, he has a garage at the back. Madge saw him drive off about an hour ago.'

'Do you happen to know where he works?'

'He's a trouble shooter for one of the supermarkets, dealing with complaints and compensation issues; he's often away for a few days at a time and out in the evenings on his own. The bloody man will use the lift when he comes back late at night; dammit, he's no great age and fit enough and could easily go up the stairs. Anyway, it's against the generally accepted rule, and it always wakes Madge up and she can't get off again.'

Sarah turned towards Mrs Forbes and gave her a smile. 'That must be pretty maddening.'

'It is and it happened again last night — I could have strangled him. I knew what I was in for directly I saw him drive off at about six. I keep telling Alec that he ought to cut the power to the lift every night at eleven, but of course he can't — health and safety and all that.'

'What time did he get back?'

'Just after midnight; I remember looking at

the time on my clock radio when I heard the lift stop at the floor which we share, so it must have been him.'

'Is he married?'

'Oh, yes, but the poor woman is like a frightened rabbit and hardly ever goes out. After he was banned from driving, he made her ferry him about, but although throughout that year she always went out with him when he needed the car, I don't believe that she did all the driving, despite what he said. I just can't see her on a motorway, particularly in that vehicle of his — it's more like a lorry than a car. I tried to get to know her when they first arrived here by asking her up for tea or coffee, but talking to her was like pulling teeth and as we were never asked back and Robert was always so rude to Alec, I gave up.'

'The remains of any relationship I had with Cahill disintegrated completely when he saw me at the court case,' Forbes said. 'Up to then, he would at least say good morning to me.'

'And from what you said, he must have felt the same about Professor Vaughan.'

'More than that. He hated her. It was a mixture of things: in her presence, he blustered even more than usual, so much so that at times could hardly get his words out, and if there was a disagreement about anything at the block's meetings, it was never a contest. Always with the facts right there and with her arguments logical and clearly articulated, she had him on toast. He never seemed to learn by experience and every lie and exaggeration was mercilessly exposed.' The man suddenly paused. 'I know what you must be thinking, but no, there's no way it could have been him, he wouldn't have had the bottle. I know about these things, you see. I was in the SAS.'

'Do you know Helen Vaughan's house-keeper?'

'Not at all, but Madge here does a bit.'

'A bit is the right word,' his wife said. 'She very much keeps herself to herself and she's never had anyone to visit her here as far as I know. There are some lovely walks around here on the Common and in Cannizaro Park, but she obviously doesn't go to either of them much or at all and mostly she just takes the buses to Putney or Wimbledon for food shopping — there are stops for both of them very close by. I asked her when she first came here if she was settling in well and it soon became quite clear that Helen frightened the daylights out of her, telling her that absolute discretion was required of her and that included never discussing anything to

42

do with her work or private life with any of the residents.'

'That sounds a bit extreme,' Sarah said.

'Yes, Helen was like that. I asked her once if she had any family and she gave me one of her mirthless smiles and said she was quite sure that that would be of no interest to anyone here.'

'Mrs Crawford told us about weekend visitors. Did you see any of them?'

'No, I think Helen must have fetched them from the station in her car. She had a double garage with an electric up-and-over door behind the block and that meant she would have come in by the back entrance. Mrs Crawford hasn't had much luck here. Alec was in the hall once when she came out of the lift with Robert Cahill.'

'Oh, what happened?'

'I think I'd better leave that to Alec,' the woman said with a smile.

'Let me just say,' the colonel said with a guffaw, 'that Robert's left cheek must have been on the receiving end of an almighty slap. I suppose the silly bugger must have tried to feel her up, or something. Admittedly she could be quite attractive if she made more of an effort, but you've met her, Inspector, and must have seen that she doesn't and also know the type of woman she is, so can you imagine the man being such a fool?'

Sarah let that one pass. 'What about Mrs Crawford's predecessor? Did you know her, Mrs Forbes?'

'Helen inherited old Mrs Cassidy from the previous owner of the flat. She was a nice old thing, but she wasn't up to the secretarial work that Helen required when she took on the administration of the block and in any case, her arthritis was getting her down and the last straw was when she had a nasty fall and broke her arm badly. She lives in sheltered accommodation in the village and I take her out for a coffee or a cup of tea from time to time.'

After thanking the old couple for their help, the two detectives stood for a moment on the landing.

'Why don't I have a quick word with Mrs Cahill?' Sarah said. 'From what the gallant colonel said she might be less frightened by a woman on her own.'

'Good idea. I'll wait for you upstairs and in the meantime give Tyrrell a call.'

There was a long pause after Sarah rang the bell of flat seven and then the door was opened on its chain.

'Yes, who is it?'

'I'm a police officer,' Sarah said, holding her warrant card in the gap. 'There's nothing for you to worry about, I'm just letting everyone in the block know that we will be coming in here quite often and to explain about Professor Vaughan. I've just been in to see Colonel and Mrs Forbes about it.'

'I don't understand. Has something happened to her?'

'May I come in?'

The woman, Sarah thought, must have been in her late thirties or early forties and would have been quite attractive had she not had an almost hunted expression on her face.

'You obviously haven't heard?'

'Heard what?'

'I'm afraid that the professor is dead; she was murdered last night.'

For one moment, Sarah thought that the woman was going to faint. She had gone ashen white and as her right hand went up to her mouth, the short sleeve of her dress rode up and Sarah saw a livid purple bruise on her upper arm.

'It didn't happen here, did it?'

'No, at the hospital where she worked.'

The woman let out her breath very slowly and a little colour began to come into her cheeks. 'I know it's silly but I get very nervous and for one moment I had the thought that the murderer might still be lurking in the block, or wandering around when I was in bed last night.'

'No wonder you're upset — I would be, too, in your shoes. Wasn't your husband here, then?'

'Yes, he was, but I get migraines and I had a terrible one last night. I'm still not over it completely and it does strange things to me; you may not believe it, but I suddenly had the ridiculous thought just now that Robert might have gone out and left me when I was asleep and alone at the mercy of some maniac.'

'Didn't your husband look in to see if you were all right before he went to bed himself?'

'No. He knows that I prefer to be left in peace when I'm in the grip of a really bad attack and he has always respected my wishes in that regard. My mother always used to make a great fuss about it before I was married, always looking in and offering me this and that pill or a hot drink. She meant well, of course, but it didn't help in the least — if anything it made it worse.'

'Is your husband away often?'

'Quite often, but not for very long. You see, he works for a chain of supermarkets and travels about the country trouble shooting at the various stores; he also quite frequently goes to meetings in London as well.'

*   *   *

'Sorry I was so long,' Sarah said when she went back up the stairs some twenty minutes later, 'but I think it was worth it. I'm quite sure that the woman knew that her husband was out last night, but she is desperately afraid of him and may well have made up the story she told me of being in bed with a migraine and out for the count the whole evening. She's got good reason to be scared of him, too; she has a nasty bruise on her upper arm and I fear for her if he believes that she has told tales about him.'

'Hmm. He sounds a right bastard and it's a good thing that Mrs Forbes gave us the low-down on him first.'

'Any luck with Tyrrell?'

'Yes, he wants us to join him for a visit to Tredgold tomorrow morning and then come back here afterwards to see what Pocock has turned up.'

'Did he say anything about his interview with McKenzie?'

'Just that the man didn't say all that much, but he got the distinct impression that although McKenzie obviously respected Helen Vaughan's professional abilities, there was not a great deal of love lost between the two of them. As to the others, he thinks that the only

47

other one worth following up is McKenzie's second-in-command, one Richard Spencer. Evidently Tyrrell got the impression that the man was holding something back. He also told me that Spencer was a funny little man and as he does practically all the post mortems, thought that it would be worth sounding Tredgold out about him, feeling sure that he would have come across him. He had and evidently was at his most waspish, not only calling Spencer a nasty little tick and an inveterate gossip, but labelling him a proper 'Uriah Creep'!'

'I can't wait to meet him,' Sarah said after she had got over her fit of the giggles.

'You won't have to wait long. Tyrrell wants us to have a detailed chat with the man and has made an appointment for him to see us at the Yard at nine o'clock on Wednesday morning. He thinks that not only is that likely to make him feel important, but he might well say more if he is away from the hospital.'

4

Tredgold was at his most acerbic when the three detectives arrived at his laboratory.

'This'll test your culinary skills, Miss Tombs. One visitor presents no problem, I've known you cope with two, but three — now that is a challenge indeed.'

'I think I'm just about up to it, sir.'

'Nil desperandum, eh, Miss Tombs, that's the spirit. Now, no holding back on the chocolate Bath Olivers and don't threaten me yet again with that idiot of a cardiologist — he doesn't know what he's talking about.'

When the woman came back, Tredgold peered at the tray over the top of his half-moon spectacles.

'I thought I told you not to hold back, Miss Tombs. Do you seriously consider that just one biscuit each is adequate sustenance for the important discussions ahead?'

'There's only one more left, sir.'

'Had I not known that you are an ascetic, who exists on locusts and wild honey, I might have suspected you of hoarding it for your own use. That idea is, of course, ridiculous, so bring it in, Miss Tombs, bring it in; I know from experience that this young lady here does not share your dietary inhibitions.'

Mark Sinclair fully expected Sarah to blush scarlet, but she did no such thing when Miss Tombs offered her the biscuit, accepting it with grateful thanks. And was it a wink that the woman gave her as she proffered it on a silver salver?

'Now,' Tredgold said, when they had finished their coffee, 'the autopsy. The cause of death is quite clear. A blow was delivered to the left side of the head with a heavy, blunt object with sufficient force to cause an open fracture of the temporal bone and severe damage to the underlying brain and in my opinion would have resulted in instant death. It is likely that the perpetrator was right-handed and that the assailant was standing in front of the victim. The positioning of the desk and chair were such that it would have been impossible for the blow to have been directed from behind. The victim must have been taken completely by surprise, making no attempt to ward it off with her hand or arm, both of which were uninjured.'

'Would the murderer's clothes have been contaminated by blood, or any other material?'

'Probable, but not certain.'

Tyrrell nodded. 'Unfortunately the only

fingerprints were those of the victim, her secretary and the cleaner. Interestingly, though, the inner handle of the door had been wiped clear and the only prints found on the external one were those of Miss Ashby.'

'So none of Professor Vaughan's was on either handle?'

'No.'

'I see.' The pathologist glanced down at his notes, then looked up at the three detectives with a quizzical expression on his face. 'It may interest you to know that there were two other findings that may present problems for you and your superiors with regard to confidentiality. Firstly, she had had a pregnancy, likely to have been carried to term, although a long time ago, and secondly, some time within one to two weeks of her death, she was on the receiving end of a caning on the buttocks. In my view, the regularity of the spacing of the bruising and the fact that there were six, suggests that it was received voluntarily. Oh, by the way, she had blue eyes and light-coloured skin, but her head hair and eyebrows had been dyed black and probably touched up recently and before you ask, her body hair had not and was very fair.'

'Hmm,' said Tyrrell, 'those findings certainly put the cat amongst the pigeons. The inquest will, of course, have to be delayed and, as the commissioner is already involved, I'll have to spend most of my time liaising with him over press releases and so on, while my two colleagues here will be in charge on the ground, although they will be keeping me in touch with any developments. I can't emphasize enough, though, that what you have told us just now, Eric, is highly sensitive. I know that none of you will take this in the wrong way, but we can't afford any leaks.'

Tredgold nodded. 'You may have no concerns about this end of the business, I can assure you.'

★   ★   ★

When the two detectives were back in the car, Sinclair gave Pocock a call and for several minutes listened to what he had to say without interrupting.

'I see,' he said, when the man had finished. 'We'll be with you in about forty-five minutes provided the traffic's reasonable.' The detective replaced the receiver and turned towards his colleague. 'It sounds as if he's found some things of interest in the locked area, but Pocock being Pocock, he's not prepared to give any details over the phone and quite right, too.'

When they arrived in Wimbledon, the scene-of-crime man was waiting for them on the landing of the fifth floor, outside Professor Vaughan's front door.

'I've replaced everything as I found it and all the details are here,' he said, handing over the typed list. 'I haven't had time to look at the garage yet, but it shouldn't take long and I'll be able to answer any queries you may have when I come back up.'

After the man had gone down in the lift, the two detectives stopped in the side corridor of the flat by the door with the key pad.

'I don't suppose he'll tell us his trade secrets,' Sinclair said as he opened it, 'but it's clear that he's managed to discover the code rather than having to force it.'

A couple of paces beyond it and to the right was a large and well-appointed bath-room with bath, basin, bidet and lavatory and a power shower in a separate cubicle. Nothing out of the ordinary had been discovered in there, but the same could not have been said of the bedroom, the entrance to which was through another door at the end of the short corridor.

'Good grief!' Sarah said. 'This is some bedroom.'

It was, being at least twenty-four feet or so

long and fourteen feet wide with windows on the east and south sides. The king-sized bed was neatly made up and against the wall with the door in it, there were ceiling-high cupboards all with locks on them. Two of them were standing open to reveal a large safe in one and a rack of costumes on hangers set on rails in the other. On top of the desk on the opposite side was a telephone with an elaborate answer machine and a TV set with a DVD player and tape recorder under it. Further along was a dressing table and three-piece mirror and finally, opposite the bed and under the south window; was a large chest of drawers.

Sinclair consulted the extensive notes that Pocock had given him and pointed at the answer machine.

'This set-up has a separate number from the others in the hall and study and it shares it with the instrument in the sun room above and he has set it to play back the call which he considers the most significant. Most if not all the calls on this extension have been recorded on cassettes and he has not had time to analyze the others, which are all here in this drawer. The call in question was made on a Thursday evening some three months ago at 22.19.'

Sinclair pressed the play button and the

voices, although slightly distorted, came through quite clearly.

'Yes.'

'It's me.'

'Not again.'

'It'll be the last time, I promise.'

'I've heard that one before.'

'It really is. I've just got a job as PA to Carl Schreiber at RSK Electronics.'

'Don't tell me, there's a snag, isn't there? The same old thing, I suppose. Had one last flutter to try to recoup your losses, did you? I want the plain unvarnished truth. How much were they?'

There was a long pause. 'I need 10K and in cash.'

'Exactly that?'

'A bit less.'

'How much less?'

'A few hundred.'

'Explain.'

'I needed some new kit for the interview — I'd never have got the job if I'd turned up looking like a typist, now would I? I put what it all cost on my credit card and went to the club to recoup enough to pay off that and the rest of my debts.'

'I see. And it all went wrong — as usual. Now, if I were to give you what you're asking for, you do realize that that will be it?'

'I know.'

'You must also know by now that I always say what I mean and that there is a price to be paid.'

There was a long pause. 'How many?'

'Ten and with number two.'

'What? Not ten, please. That's too many.'

'One per thousand. That's fair, isn't it? Saturday week at 5 p.m. is the earliest I can offer you. If you can't face it, you're on your own — for good.'

'But . . . '

'No buts and I need your decision now.'

There was an even longer pause.

'All right,' the woman said in a hoarse whisper.

'And don't forget, that really will be that. No more bailings out and it's up to you to stick to that job.'

There was a loud click and Sinclair switched off the machine.

'What on earth's all that about?' Sarah asked.

'There's a note from Pocock here to say that there is a video camera and tripod in that cupboard over there and he's set up the relevant cassette at the right place for us in the recorder in the sitting room; there's a plasma screen in there, which you probably saw before. I gather that the first section he suggests we look at is dated just over three months ago, ten days after the phone call we just listened to, and the second two weeks ago.'

When they had moved through to the sitting room, Sinclair adjusted the blinds and pressed the play button on the recorder. A woman with shoulder-length blonde hair, who was wearing a flowered dress, came into view and stood in front of the camera, head bowed.

'You know why you're here?' came a voice off camera.

'Yes.'

'And you accept your punishment.' The woman nodded. 'I want to hear you say it.'

'I accept my punishment.'

'Take it bravely without getting up, you'll get your money and that'll be the end of it. This is your last chance and by now you'll know that I always mean exactly what I say.'

The ordeal began and Sarah winced at every stroke.

'My God!' said Sinclair when he had put the machine on hold. 'I've heard about this sort of thing, but the reality is very difficult to stomach. I don't suppose there's much chance of it being faked.'

'I'm sure it's not,' Sarah said. 'It looked mighty convincing to me.'

'The next section is also one that Pocock thinks we ought to see — he's fairly sure that Helen Vaughan was the victim that time. He recognized her from her passport photo.'

The table was in the same position, but the woman who came into view was shorter and slimmer than the previous one and had shoulder-length dark hair, which was largely covered by a black mortar board. She was wearing a black academic gown over her dress and was staring at the woman who had carried out the punishment in the previous episode, who was in a white shirt and navy blue pinafore and was standing on the other side.

'I understand that you swore at Miss Harper, using language which would have disgraced even a navvy. What have you got to say for yourself?'

'She was humiliating me in front of the other girls by making fun of my French accent and I lost my temper.'

'Well, we'll just have to make sure that not only does your accent improve, but that you never do anything like that again.'

The 'schoolgirl' was much thinner than the previous victim had been and Sarah felt herself blushing scarlet at what she could see as the punishment was carried out, six strokes delivered from above shoulder height, leaving a pattern of evenly spaced scarlet weals.

'Perhaps we ought to get Pocock to ask the audio-visual people to clean up the images of the faces of the three different women we've seen in the video,' said Sarah.

'Good idea. Perhaps I ought to see that man Cahill now and would you feel strong enough to do a quick trawl through the other videos and the tapes on the answer machine and see what you can find out from Helen Vaughan's personal documents, bank statements and so on?'

★ ★ ★

Sarah knew only too well that if she had had to tell anyone other than Jack Pocock that she wanted a list of the contents of the various tapes and was intending to view a selection of them, it would have been all over the Yard within a matter of hours. Having worked with him on a number of occasions before, though, she knew that, strange and taciturn though the man was, she would be able to trust him completely. She found him in the bedroom, standing by an anonymous-looking man who was kneeling in front of the substantial safe.

'There's only been time to skim through these,' he said, pointing to the pile of video tapes on top of the desk, 'but I do have a list of the various titles and subtitles, which will give you an idea of what's in them. Most of the clothes in there,' he said, pointing to the other open cupboard, 'have been used as props. There are also some still photographs on the laptop, which you might care to have a look at. Would you like me to set it up together with the tapes in the sitting room and then you'll be able to study them at your leisure?'

'Yes, please.'

Sarah ran her eye down the list and saw that they were almost all on the same general theme of lesbianism and what was called female discipline. The only one she had heard of was a mainstream film called *The Story of O*.

It took her over an hour to run through the domestic tape, despite liberal use of the fast-forward button. Helen was in several scenes, most of which involved the tall woman with the blonde wig — although, on account of the different accents the women had used and the costumes they had worn, it was difficult to be absolutely certain.

'I've got everything I want from these,' Sarah said when she returned the whole collection to Pocock, 'but it's possible that Tyrrell will want to review them himself.'

'Right, I'll lock them up where they were

before. He'll need a code to access the still pictures on the laptop and I'm keeping that to myself for the time being. By the way, as you can see, we managed to get that safe open and you might like to look through the contents and the financial statements.'

Sarah had always thought that the scene-of-crime man disapproved of female police officers. It was not as if he had ever made remarks to that effect, it was just his manner that seemed to radiate it. Now, she suddenly understood that she had just been paranoid, realizing that Pocock was the same with everyone and was desperately shy. The fact was, though, that he had been very sensitive over the tapes and pictures — most of the other men she had worked with would have taken that opportunity to make coarse remarks and embarrass her.

Her first surprise was to find that there was no evidence of Helen Vaughan having taken any large sums out of her bank current account, or transfers from her e-savings account, which had a credit balance of a little over £50,000 in it, or her mini cash ISAs. Her second was that there were two wills, one dated eighteen months previously, in which she had left everything — apart from a bequest for genome research at Cambridge University and £20,000 to one Jean Redman, whose address was in New Malden — to Emily Dickinson — care of a firm of Wimbledon solicitors, one of the partners being named as sole executor. The second, this time drawn up by a different firm of solicitors only six weeks previously, was the same except that the bequest to Jean Redman had been taken out and there was a different executor. A rough calculation was enough to make it clear that the sums involved were likely to have been substantial. Helen Vaughan had a high salary, which comfortably covered overheads, mainly community and maintenance charges for the flat and payment of the housekeeper, and there was no evidence of mortgage payments. True, she did not appear to have much in the way of investments, just some capital investment bonds, but the flat alone, Sarah thought, must have been worth at least three quarters of a million.

In the safe, apart from the will, there was some costume jewellery, Helen Vaughan's passport and two photographs. One of them was of a man and a woman with a blonde girl aged about ten standing on a beach. They were all wearing bathing costumes and the man, who was almost completely bald, had his hand resting on the child's shoulder. The other one was of another girl, also fair-haired;

she was in her teens, wearing school uniform. Comparing the two, although there were obvious similarities, Sarah was almost certain that they were not of the same person and might well have been sisters.

★   ★   ★

Mark Sinclair decided to study the file that Pocock had found concerning the case at the magistrates' court before tackling Cahill, but after reassuring himself that the man's car was still on the forecourt, he wasn't going to run the risk of him disappearing and rang him up.

'Mr Cahill?'

'Yes.'

'My name is Sinclair, Inspector Sinclair. You've no doubt heard the distressing news about Professor Vaughan and that we have begun our enquiries here.'

'That's nothing to do with me.'

'Nevertheless, there are a number of points I'd like to clairfy with you. Shall we say three o'clock this afternoon in your flat?'

'That's not convenient.'

'In that case, perhaps you'd prefer me to arrange for a police car to collect you and take you to our station at Wimbledon.'

'I . . . I . . . '

'Three o'clock it is, then.'

The policeman hadn't raised his voice at all, but there had been a definite edge to it and Cahill was both agitated and in a foul mood when his wife brought in a tray with his lunch on it.

'What's this?' he said, stabbing his fork down hard.

'It's a poached egg on toast, which is what you asked me to get you.'

'I know it's a bloody poached egg, but it's an overcooked poached egg with the yolk like plastic. Bring me another and get it right this time.'

If Carole was responsible for having told the fuzz about the court case, he'd . . . She had denied it, of course, and also assured him that she had told them that he had been in for the entire Sunday evening.

Somehow, he managed to get through the long wait before the policeman was due and was hanging about in the hall when there was a sharp ring on the bell. Even though he ought to have expected it from the man's voice, he was still thrown by his appearance. He could have coped with a bullet-headed thug with an aggressively short haircut, bursting out of an ill-fitting blue serge suit, but the tall, slim, immaculately dressed man with the cultivated accent and firm handshake was deeply unsettling.

'How can I help you?' he said, when they were sitting in one of the bedrooms, which had been converted into a study with a laptop, printer, TV, video recorder and DVD player.

'You must know by now that Professor Vaughan was murdered in her office at the City Hospital last Sunday evening.'

'Yes, it was on TV last night.'

'Would you mind telling me where you were between the hours of seven and midnight on the night it happened?'

'Why do you want to know?'

'I understand that you had a problem with the professor after you were found guilty of careless driving eighteen months ago.'

Cahill could feel his heart beginning to pound. 'It was that stupid young woman's fault. She was coming down the hill far too fast and ran straight into the back of my car.'

'That does not appear to have been the conclusion of the court.'

'That was unfair and if it hadn't been for that Vaughan woman, the right person would have been blamed and that was that silly girl who should never have passed her test.'

'I also believe that you used threatening language to Professor Vaughan when you had a disagreement with her at one of the maintenance company's meetings here.'

'So, that pompous ass Forbes has been speaking to you, has he? I momentarily lost my temper — so what? Anyway, if you must know, I was here with my wife all the evening in question. She had one of her migraines and I watched TV. She will confirm it if you don't believe me.'

'It's not a question of what I believe, sir, because you need to explain the fact that you were observed leaving the block in your car at about 7.30 and heard coming back up in the lift a few minutes after midnight.'

Cahill had no time to think, except that it must have been that bastard Forbes, or even more likely his fat-arsed wife who had told the detective, and felt the sweat breaking out on his forehead.

'I went to a club, if you must know.'

'I see. Its name?'

'The Blue Elephant.'

'And what sort of club would that be?'

'Lap dancing.'

'And were you there for the best part of five hours?'

'If you must know, I went to a hotel with one of the girls when she had finished her stint.'

'When exactly was that?'

'It must have been at about 10.30.'

'How long were you with her?'

'About an hour.'

'And which particular young lady would that have been?'

'I don't know her name.'

'You'll have to do better than that. I will have to check on your story and for that I require the address of the club, the names of the girl and the hotel, as well as an up-to-date photograph of yourself. I also require you to come down to Wimbledon station and sign a statement, confirming what you have just told me and it would also be wise for you to arrange for your solicitor to be present.'

The detective made a gesture towards the telephone and after a moment's hesitation, Cahill shook his head. The only contacts he had had with solicitors had been over the conveyancing of his flat and after the incident with his car and he liked them about as much as he liked policemen. Once one of them started to poke into his affairs, there might be no end to it.

'Will I have to stay there?'

'That won't be necessary, but you will be required to report there every day until our enquiries have been completed.'

'You won't have to tell my wife, will you?'

'Not if what you have told me is confirmed.'

'I may not have liked Helen, but I would never have done her any harm.'

'Shall we go?'

★ ★ ★

Sarah had just got up from Helen Vaughan's desk and was massaging her neck, when Mark Sinclair came in to the bedroom.

'Looks bad,' he said, giving her a smile.

'It is. I don't know about you, but I've had it up to here for today.'

'Me, too.' Sinclair glanced at his watch. 'How about a meal? There must be a decent hostelry somewhere near here and if I promise not to bore you with that sleazeball Cahill, you needn't bore me with what you've been up to here.'

'It's a deal.'

Two hours later, a combination of the tapes and photographs she had seen that day, the excellent meal, most of a bottle of red wine and the company of an amusing and undeniably attractive man produced the most direct and embarrassing effects on Sarah's physiology. It was almost as if someone else was speaking when she suddenly said:

'Why don't we go back to my place for a cup of coffee?'

For one awful moment, she thought she

had made the most monumental miscalculation, but then he raised his eyebrows and grinned at her.

'What a good idea!'

It was only when she was in the bath the following morning after Mark had gone back to his flat to shave and freshen up before their meeting with Spencer at the Yard, that Sarah really took in what had happened the previous evening and the way she had behaved.

She remembered going into her flat with him and then . . . Then, there was only a confused recollection of images and sensations. Had her fingers really gone straight to the belt of his trousers almost before the door had closed behind them and had she then been wrestled over his knee, with him sitting on the sofa, and then had there been the staccato crack as his hand came down? Had it been the fashionable endorphins, or even the unaccustomed alcohol she had drunk at dinner, or even the sublimation of a long repressed fantasy? Whatever the reason, as it continued, there had been no unpleasant pain, just a spreading warmth into the very centre of her. At times taking the initiative and at times being on the receiving end of previously unknown experiences, she vaguely remembered crying out as she fell into the abyss; there were a few moments of boneless relaxation in his arms and then she had fallen into dreamless sleep.

Sarah got out of the bath, wiped the condensation off the mirror and looked at herself over her shoulder. Her bottom was pink like the rest of her, but there was no trace of any bruising, nor was there any swelling or tenderness of the more delicate areas of her body. That hadn't been the end of it, either; she had been woken just as it was getting light by him making love to her again, this time very slowly and gently, which was just as satisfying.

What had got into her? As soon as she had the thought, she knew perfectly well what the answer was; although she had found some of the things in the videos disturbing and even distasteful, the same wasn't true of a lot of them, particularly the bits she had re-run at the end. She had fondly hoped that by the time Mark had come back after she had returned the videos to Pocock and spent some time looking through Helen Vaughan's papers, her excitement and arousal would no longer have been obvious, but quite clearly that had not been the case. She remembered the hint of a smile on his face as he had looked at her when he came into Helen

Vaughan's bedroom and the almost imperceptible raising of his eyebrows.

She knew very little about Sinclair except that like Tyrrell, he had been to Oxford University. The fact that the two toffs were working together was a standing joke at the Yard, but if being a toff meant being polite, well-mannered and sensitive, she was all for it. She was well aware that the two things didn't by any means go together; her stepfather, a clergyman, had been equally well educated, but anyone more self-centred and mean-spirited, she could hardly imagine. One thing was certain, though, she thought as she felt herself blushing: getting to know the man better was going to be an experience and a half.

5

Richard Spencer didn't approve of radio alarm clocks. Whatever was on them, be it music, an interview or a commentary, was a distraction to the serious business of getting up, which he did without fail at 7.00 a.m. seven days a week. That type of clock wasn't accurate enough, either, nothing like his new one, which was linked to the National Physics Laboratory signal transmitted from Rugby and was correct to within one second in a million years. Not only that, the change from British winter to summer time in the spring and the reverse in the autumn was carried out automatically, so no worry there.

His morning bath took precisely fifteen minutes, which included scouring it afterwards and rinsing it carefully with a jet from the showerhead so that there would be no trace left of the cleaning powder. After putting on fresh underwear and a dressing gown, his next port of call was the kitchen where he boiled the brown, free-range egg for precisely four minutes, twenty-three seconds, measured by his stopwatch, then ground the Colombian coffee beans, put them into the percolator, and while it was operating, put two slices of harvest grain bread into the toaster.

The egg was perfect, the white perfectly set, the yolk just running, and when he had finished it he wiped his lips delicately with the linen napkin and after toast, organic butter and Frank Cooper's marmalade, washed up, then went back into the bathroom to shave and clean his teeth.

Spencer remembered with absolute clarity what the tall, softly spoken, but none the less authoritative detective superintendent had said after they had been talking about the department for several minutes.

'You obviously have an impressive grasp of detail and knowledge of this department and I wish I had time to benefit from it now. Would it be possible for you to come to Scotland Yard at, say, nine o'clock tomorrow morning to discuss it further with my two assistants, who are already playing a most important part in the investigation of this tragic affair. I judge it wise not to arrange it here — people might get the wrong impression, I'm sure you would agree.'

'Indeed I do, Superintendent. It's most thoughtful of you, if I may say so. I will be there without fail.'

Spencer arrived at Scotland Yard at

precisely the time stated and felt a warm glow of satisfaction when he wasn't kept waiting and was taken straight up to meet the two detectives.

'Thank you for coming, Dr Spencer,' the pleasant-looking, slightly plump and fresh-faced young woman said after she had introduced herself and her male colleague. 'Would you care for a cup of coffee?'

'That would be very acceptable, very acceptable indeed.'

It wasn't instant coffee, either; if he was any judge it was Brazilian and freshly ground. That wasn't all: there were also crisp ginger biscuits. The superintendent he had seen briefly at the hospital had been obviously cultured, urbane and immaculately turned out. He found it a little disappointing that the man wasn't present now, but the two inspectors were, to his eyes, almost as acceptable, both being scrupulously polite and well spoken.

'It would be very helpful to us, Dr Spencer,' Inspector Sinclair said, 'if you would give us an idea of how the pathology department is organized.'

Spencer was in his element and paused for a moment to collect his thoughts.

'There are four sections in the department,' he said, 'morbid anatomy, chemical pathology, haematology and bacteriology. I mention morbid anatomy first because not only do I have the privilege of working in it, but Professor McKenzie is both the head of this section and that of the whole department. He and I are responsible for the immediate reporting on specimens taken at operation, on which very often decisions have to be taken about the need for and extent of surgery, and nowadays I do all the autopsies, except, of course, when I am on holiday, when the professor takes over.'

'What about research in your section?'

It was not a question that Spencer had been expecting, but it gave him an opportunity he was not going to miss.

'You would no doubt think that the professor would combine clinical work, teaching, administration and research, wouldn't you, but in all truth, Alastair is not and has never been a research worker and he was only made a professor because at that time the university side was expanding and he happened to be the senior man. It was that side of things more than anything else that created the tension between him and Helen Vaughan.'

'So they didn't get on?'

'I am quite sure that you wouldn't want me to pretend otherwise. Alastair is one of the old school, who is invariably polite and courteous, and Helen unsettled him profoundly. If there was a controversy, she was almost always right and combined that with brutal directness and then, too, there was the brilliance of her research. Soon after arriving at the City, she was awarded a personal chair; a fellowship of the Royal Society was bound to follow and even a Nobel prize was not beyond the bounds of possibility. Let me give you an example. You will understand, of course, that what I am about to tell you is in the strictest confidence.'

★   ★   ★

Spencer remembered the scene as if it had been the day before. In years gone by, the appointment of senior house officers to the various sections of the department of pathology had been virtually within the gift of the head of that section, but for some time, every appointment had become more formal in order to make it fairer, and certainly the question of possible discrimination against women had been an important factor as well.

The post in question was for haematology and both Helen Vaughan and Ashton, as consultants in that section, were on the committee as well as Alastair McKenzie, Spencer and Fellowes, the other two senior men in the department. On examination results alone, there were two candidates — one man and one woman — well ahead of the others, and another young woman, who, to Spencer's eyes, was a good deal weaker than the other two, and those three had been selected for interview.

The first young woman interviewed very well, rather better than the man, although there was not much to choose between the two of them on examination results alone, and then it came to the third candidate, Rebecca Turner. Helen Vaughan had fixed her with her laser-like eyes, then there was a pause, which was just long enough to enhance the young woman's already obvious anxiety and then came the first question in her deceptively quiet voice.

'Would you tell the committee why you wish to obtain this post?'

It was generally understood that at least one of those junior posts in pathology went to the best young doctors in order to give them an insight into the various sub-disciplines in addition to that of the section to which they were formally attached, before they went on to a career in medicine and surgery. This was just such an occasion, the other posts already having been filled by those wanting to specialize in pathology. Rebecca Turner must have known this, but she nevertheless launched into an obviously prepared speech about her fascination with haematology and DNA testing and research in particular.

Helen Vaughan was icily polite, but tied the young woman up in knots, who obviously had not the slightest idea how to extricate herself. McKenzie had intervened and did his considerable best to pick up the pieces, getting her to go through her good exam results, which although perfectly reasonable, were, in fact, also no match for the other two.

In the summing up, Helen began by saying that perhaps they could all agree that the last candidate was by far the weakest of the three and went as far as to remark, somewhat acidly, that she was surprised that the young woman had even been shortlisted. With the notable exception of Alastair, there were nods of approval when she suggested that she should not be considered further.

'I don't think that's fair,' McKenzie said. 'Rebecca Turner's not had the advantages of a private education like the other two and she is the only one to have been to this medical school. I'm not saying that we should always choose people on that basis, but I think we should do so on this occasion. I have been concerned for some time that there is a bias against our own graduates and this cannot be a good thing. If we seriously believe that our home-grown young doctors are not good enough, what is that going to do for the standards of our intake?'

'That is a valid point and I don't doubt that Miss Turner is an intelligent young woman,' Helen replied, 'but it is glaringly obvious that she is immature, young for her age and unlike the other candidates failed to take a gap year between school and coming here. If she had been advised to do that at the interview at which she was given a place as a pre-clinical student, it would have done her a power of good. I also understand that she had to take some time off for a stress-related disorder during her surgical house job and as that post was in the provinces and she was not considered good enough to obtain one here, it is difficult to see how anyone could prefer her over obviously better candidates, particularly the other young woman who interviewed outstandingly well.'

McKenzie did his best for Rebecca Turner, saying that he had heard that she had only been off work for two weeks with a flu-like illness and that it wasn't fair to bring that up. In reply to that, Helen Vaughan gave one of her mirthless smiles and an almost imperceptible shake of her head, also pointing out that the candidate she favoured, Fiona Grant, had even better grades, had been active in her medical school's extra-curricular activities, particularly with regard to music, and in her gap year had worked with AIDS sufferers in Zambia. It had been no contest and with obvious reluctance McKenzie gave way.

★ ★ ★

'Why do you suppose Professor McKenzie supported that young woman so strongly? It seems clear from your account that she didn't match up to the successful candidate in any way, not to mention the man.'

'I don't know. Perhaps it was just that Helen got on Alastair's nerves and that had the effect of warping his judgement. Anyway, after that episode, the two of them were hardly on speaking terms.'

'That seems a rather excessive reaction, particularly on his part.'

'I should have explained; the evening following that committee meeting, the young woman, Rebecca Turner, killed herself by cutting her wrists.'

'What a terrible thing!' Sarah said.

'Yes it was and I believe that Alastair blamed Helen for it, although he never said so to her face.'

'And how did Professor Vaughan react?'

'I never discussed the incident with her myself, but one of my colleagues told me that she had been very sorry to hear about it, but that the real fault lay with the medical school authorities who should have picked up at her initial interview the fact that the young woman was not psychologically robust enough for a career in medicine.'

'Have you any idea who is likely to succeed Professor Vaughan?'

Spencer shook his head. 'It's going to be very difficult. I think it likely that teams working on DNA research in other institutions will poach the best people from Helen's former department and then, when Alastair retires, attempts will be made to set up a new professorial team in some other line of research in pathology.'

'Do you know anything about Helen Vaughan's personal life?'

'Nothing at all. She never came to any of the social gatherings here and I can't think of anyone who liked her. Respected, yes, but liked, no.'

'Did you share that view yourself?'

'I don't judge people I don't know and her interests in the hospital and medical school were totally different from mine.'

'In what way?'

'As I've already indicated, Helen was

totally dedicated to her research and I have few talents in that direction. Providing a good clinical service and teaching the students is what I enjoy doing and I like to think that I make a good job of both.'

'How about the others in the department?'

'They are all highly competent, but I wouldn't say that any of them are outstanding in their respective fields.'

'Are you friends with any of them? Socially, I mean?'

'Hospitals and medical schools have changed a great deal in recent years, what with amalgamations and a great increase in the number of female students. In days gone by, the consultants took a considerable interest in student activities, everything from music to games, and were often seen in their club, but all that has changed. To give you an example, I was president of the chess club a few years ago and used to play with the students regularly, but then it closed through lack of interest. It's all boyfriend/girlfriend now.'

'For the better, do you think?'

'One has to adjust to changing times and now I keep my social life strictly apart from my professional one.' He looked at Sarah and gave her a hint of a smile. 'I know that must sound pompous, but it's not meant to be.'

'I don't think it sounds pompous at all. We're very grateful to you for coming; it's given us a much clearer idea of the organization of the department and some of the personalities involved.'

'If I can be of any more help, you only have to ask.'

'Thank you. We'll certainly bear that in mind.'

After one of the secretaries had shown him out, Sinclair looked down at the notes he had been making.

'I don't know about you, Sarah, but although my first impression of him was that he was a pompous, obsessional little man, I rather took to him in the end.'

'I agree. He's obviously gay and I suspect that his analysis of the pathology department is pretty accurate. Tyrrell will no doubt want to see McKenzie again and I'm intrigued by the sad story of the young woman who committed suicide.'

'So am I and that clearly needs to be looked into. Perhaps, as a start, a meeting with the dean might be a good idea.'

★ ★ ★

Harold Tranter, dean of the City Hospital's medical school, was a tall, almost completely

83

bald man, very thin and looking as if all the cares of the world were on his shoulders, which, Sinclair thought, they probably were.

'As you may imagine,' the detective said, 'we're trying to get as much background on Professor Vaughan and the pathology department as we possibly can. I understand that there were tensions between her and Professor McKenzie.'

The man on the other side of the table gave a thin, mirthless smile. 'That is certainly no secret.'

'I gather that at least some of it followed the suicide of a junior doctor by the name of Rebecca Turner, who was applying for a post in their department.'

There was a long pause. 'I don't see how that links up with Helen Vaughan's murder; after all, the girl's death occurred nearly four years ago. Anyway, if I don't tell you what happened, someone else will and those views may well be coloured by personalities and prejudice. I'd better get hold of the file.'

During the five minutes it took for the man's secretary to find it, the silence would have become progressively more oppressive had the two detectives not played that particular game themselves on a number of occasions, and they sat there perfectly relaxed until the woman came back.

Tranter studied the file for several minutes and then cleared his throat. 'Firstly,' he said, 'perhaps I'd better explain how things changed here about ten years ago. Before that, roughly half the students came straight from school to the pre-clinical medical school here for the first three years, then were joined by the other half, most of whom came from Oxbridge. The pre-clinical and clinical parts were completely separate. Almost everything was turned upside-down once the decision to introduce a fully integrated curriculum to the medical school had been taken; that meant that the students came into contact with patients right from the start of their course.

'If I had had anything to do with it at that time, which I didn't, I would have opposed it vigorously. Many, probably the majority of eighteen-year-olds, aren't, in my view, mature enough to cope with the psychological stresses that occur when they come face to face with the sick and the dying. There are plenty of people who believe that that is nonsense and refer you to the Mozarts and Pitts, but they were aberrations, if I may put it that way. In my opinion, geniuses often make very bad doctors. Helen Vaughan, if you like, was a good example of both the points I am trying to make. Cambridge was the perfect place for her to start and mature her intellectual gifts. She also had the good sense to realize at her medical school, St Gregory's, that clinical medicine as a career was not for her, but would nevertheless stand her in good stead for the research she already had in mind. I knew her reasonably well and have no doubt that she would have been a disaster as a clinician. What was different about her from many others was that she was well aware of that herself and acted upon it.

'Anyway, Rebecca Turner came straight from school with top grades in her state exams, but I'm sure you know that that doesn't mean much these days — almost all our applicants can say the same. Alastair McKenzie was dean at the time and was also chairman of the panel of three which was responsible for sifting applicants. I see here that the other two had reservations about her on the grounds that she was underweight and a bit hyperactive and expressed concern about possible anorexia. One of them suggested that she would be well advised to take a gap year, get used to life away from home and reapply at the end of that time. Alastair countered that by pointing out that the medical school was already being criticized for having too few female students and those from state schools and he won the day.'

'She must have coped well enough with the course and her exams to have qualified, though,' Sarah said.

'Yes, she did, but not without one of the staff who runs the student health service being concerned about her; there was a spell in the middle of the course when she had to have time off with worries about possible glandular fever, or ME, both of which I fear are often used as an umbrella beneath which to hide psychological flaws. There is another factor, which also happens to be a hobby-horse of mine. You see, we had also changed from a clinical exam with real patients and independent examiners at the end of the course, to continuous assessment. The latter system favours the obsessional workers, who find favour with their tutors and, dare I say it, the women. Does this new system select better doctors? I very much doubt it, but I am considered to be something of a dinosaur and there are many who will be glad to see the back of me as dean, when my term ends next year.'

'I gather that Rebecca Turner didn't get her first house jobs here,' Sinclair said.

'No, those go to the real top-notchers and she certainly wasn't one of those.'

'Did McKenzie have anything to do with the selection for those posts?'

'I don't know, but I would have thought it highly unlikely; the clinicians almost always take that on. Anyway, Rebecca Turner appears to have coped with the posts she did get in the provinces perfectly adequately, if her references from them are anything to go by. There is something of an art in writing references for someone who one feels is not up to scratch, particularly in these litigious days, and long gone is the time when consultants could get away with statements such as 'he worked for me for six months entirely to his own satisfactions'. Anyway, reading between the lines, I gather that she was conscientious to a fault, found the surgical post stressful and there were hints that she might well be advised to seek a future in a discipline, such as pathology, away from the rigours of clinical medicine. It seems to me more than likely that the person who wrote that reference, a woman, advised her accordingly and that is why Miss Turner applied for the pathology post here.'

'From what I heard, Professor McKenzie supported her strongly for it and I gather that her failure to get the job was mentioned by the coroner as being a possible factor in her suicide.'

'I hadn't heard that myself, nor is there any mention of it in this file.'

Sinclair was quite certain that the man was being 'economical with the truth'. Surely someone from the City Hospital would have been at the inquest and the event must have created waves both in the hospital and medical school.

'If that was true, and I have no reason to doubt the reliability of our informant, why do you suppose that McKenzie would have done so? After all, the post was in Professor Vaughan's section in the department and her favoured candidate had a better record and, for that matter, was also a woman.'

'I can't answer that, not having been there, nor having had any reason to ask Alastair about it, but he's a very kindly man and he may have realized that in addition to being bright, Dr Turner was getting upset and needed a boost to her morale.'

'Do you happen to know who did the post mortem on that student?'

'Yes, it was Dr Tredgold, the forensic pathologist, who has no direct connection with this hospital or medical school. You've no doubt come across him.'

'Yes,' said Sinclair, 'we have.'

They were given the name and address of Rebecca Turner's mother, her next of kin, but Dr Tranter was unable to find any reference to Helen Vaughan's family and suggested that they might try at St Gregory's Hospital Medical School, where she had done her early training.

* * *

Dr Craxton, the dean of St Gregory's, who was a rather frail-looking, soft-spoken man, got up to greet them as they were shown into his office, and the two detectives faced him from across his desk.

'Yes, I knew Helen Vaughan, quite well, in fact. She was the most brilliant student that I can remember in the nearly thirty years that I have been here. She came from Cambridge having had a glittering academic record there. She obtained a double first and won several prizes and not surprisingly when she qualified in medicine, she was given her first choice of house jobs here. At that time, the newly qualified doctors had to do a medical and surgical house job before becoming registered as a medical practitioner and those wishing to specialize in hospital medicine went in for further training in progressively more senior and responsible posts as senior house officers, registrars, senior registrars and finally consultants. Helen's first job was in surgery and she then came on to the medical firm of which I was head.

'It was immediately obvious to me that she was not cut out to be a clinician. Don't get me wrong, she was right on top of the job; I have never come across anyone who was more efficient, wrote better notes or analyzed cases better. It was just that she completely lacked empathy with the patients; she just didn't engage with them. My wife Audrey only met her once — we always liked to invite the junior staff out to dinner during their six months on the firm — and I remember that after Helen had gone, she said: 'My God, she's a pretty tough nut.'

'We had been talking about a train disaster and the long-term effects on the people who hadn't been physically injured, but who were suffering from stress disorders. The gist of what she said was that she had no patience with them; they needed to get on with their lives and should have had the good sense not to have got ensnared by psychiatrists, counsellors, or any of the other do-gooders who descended on them like a plague of locusts. I happen to believe that she had a point, but not to the extent of being so utterly uncompromising. Being Helen, though, she had all the evidence at her fingertips and even cited papers on concentration camp survivors, which showed that those who went to displaced persons' camps afterwards and had more or less to fend for themselves, did better than those, like the Danes, who had received what was thought at the time to be the very best psychological treatments available.

'To Helen's great credit, though, she knew her own shortcomings and that clinical medicine was not for her, merely a necessary adjunct to her scientific interests, which you no doubt know about.'

'But why, in that case, did she go through a long training in clinical medicine, when she already knew that she wasn't going to go into that branch?' Sarah asked.

'Money is the short answer. It has long been a bone of contention that medically qualified people in purely scientific disciplines, such as physiology, get better paid than those who are not, and one can hardly blame those like Helen Vaughan who take that into account. Apart from monetary considerations, a training in clinical medicine undoubtedly helps many lines of research and her special interest, DNA, is one of them.'

'Do you know anything about her personal background? You see, we are anxious to trace her next of kin; no one has come forward despite all the media interest.'

'I'm afraid not. I got out her personal file when I knew you were coming and there is no record of that at all.'

'Isn't that surprising?'

'Not all that; you have to remember that Helen was twenty-one when she came here as a student. She left the next-of-kin slot blank and it obviously wasn't followed up.'

'Was she close friends with any of the other students here?' Sinclair asked.

'I don't really know, but I doubt it somehow. There was no one in her year who came from the same college at Cambridge and the set-up there is much more college — than university — orientated at a social level and it's not surprising that the other Cambridge students here shouldn't have known her well. Her particular college, too, takes very few medical students. As it happens, I know Patrick Vine, who was the senior tutor there when Helen was an undergraduate, very well — he's a distant relative of mine. I'll give him a ring if you like and you can speak to him yourself.'

As soon as he started to talk to the man, Sinclair knew that they wouldn't be able to get anywhere without their going up to see him in Cambridge. He was scrupulously polite, but clearly wished to see their ID for himself and, in any case, didn't have all the information at his fingertips. However, after Sinclair had explained that they had been unable to contact Helen Vaughan's next of kin, he agreed to make himself available the following morning if they were able to meet him at the college.

'One last favour,' Sinclair said to the dean after he had rung off. 'We'd like to speak to someone here who was an exact contemporary of Helen Vaughan as a student and I was wondering if you knew anyone on the current staff who might fit the bill?'

'I can't think of anyone offhand, but I'd be surprised if there wasn't. Miss Rogers, who looks after present and past staff records, should be able to help you. I'll give her a ring right away and get her to come here and show you to her office. It's rather tucked away and I'd never be able to give you adequate instructions to find it in this rabbit warren of a place.'

'Thank you so much,' Sinclair said to him when the woman had arrived, 'you've been more than helpful.'

'Glad to have been of some use. As you may imagine this tragedy has hit all those who knew Helen here very hard, very hard indeed.'

Miss Rogers had no need of her files. 'Dr Graham Symonds is the man you need,' she said at once. 'He's one of the consultants here; his speciality is physical medicine and he came here from Oxford as a student at exactly the same time as Professor Vaughan did from Cambridge. He organizes reunions and helps me to keep details of old alumni up to date and I'm sure he'll be able to put you in touch with some of her contemporaries.'

6

Symonds agreed to see them straight away. He was, Sinclair thought, in his middle to late thirties and was tall and athletic-looking.

'Yes,' he said, 'I got to know Helen pretty well when we were students together and we also did house jobs at the same time. It was a terrible shock to hear of her death and I'd be glad to help in any way I can.'

'We'd be most grateful for that and I was also wondering if you knew any women students who might have known her. I would like to get a female view of her as well, if at all possible, and Helen might have talked to one of them about her family. You see, we're trying to trace her next of kin and so far we've had no luck.'

The man hardly paused for thought. 'Ruth Kendall would undoubtedly be your best bet. She was, I believe, the closest and, to be honest, just about the only friend of either sex that Helen had here. She's a GP in a practice in Guildford and uses her maiden name at work. Someone told me that she had a small daughter, but I don't know what her husband does. If you're able to get down there, I'm sure she'd see you. I'll give her a ring, if you like; I've got both her home and surgery numbers in the register of old alumni which is on that shelf up there and, in fact, I was in touch with her only a few weeks back about an anniversary get-together of our year. She wasn't able to come as it turned out.'

It took him only a few minutes to get through.

'Ruth? It's Graham Symonds here. You must have been as shocked as I was to hear about Helen . . . I can well understand that. Look, I've got the police here and they're trying to trace her next of kin with no luck so far. They want every bit of help they can get and I felt sure you'd be happy to have a chat with Inspector Sarah Prescott. She's quite prepared to come down to see you . . . Yes, the sooner the better. Why don't I put her on the line?'

After Sarah had introduced herself, she listened for a couple of minutes and then said: 'Just a moment and I'll have a word with my colleague here.' She put her hand over the receiver and looked across at Sinclair. 'She's got a free slot at 4.30 and I reckon I should be able to get down there in time if I leave straightaway. All right if I take the car?'

Sinclair nodded and when she had rung off, he got out of his chair. 'Would you excuse us for a moment, Dr Symonds? Some arrangements to make.'

The two detectives went out into the corridor. 'I'll give you a ring tonight, Sarah. It's something I'm not exactly looking forward to, but first I must check on Cahill's alibi and I'll also find out train times for tomorrow. Good luck in Guildford.'

'You certainly get about,' Symonds said when Mark Sinclair went back into the office.

'Yes, but rather that than being stuck in an office all day.'

The man nodded. 'You want to know about Helen? Well, how shall I put it? Are you familiar with normal distribution curves, Inspector?'

'Yes, I am.'

If the man was surprised, he managed not to show it. 'Good. Well, on the curve of male/female characteristics, Helen was a long way on the male side in practically all the parameters. In psychological terms, she was focussed, directional and single-minded with an amazing grasp of detail. The broad canvas was not for her; she honed in on a problem and was never deflected from it, having great powers of concentration. That's why she was such a good chess player, not a game most women are interested in — they don't see the point. She was also the most driven person I have ever met; everything she tackled, be it work or sport, she pursued relentlessly. By and large women bring empathy and human understanding to medicine and Helen lacked those qualities almost completely. She had little time for psychological frailty and was very much one of the 'pull yourself together', 'stop feeling sorry for yourself' school of thought. I'm not saying that she was totally devoid of sympathy and she certainly didn't lack insight. She told me she only went into medicine to further her career in research and that will give you some idea of just how driven she was. It's not everyone who is able to see through three years of clinical training and then a year's house jobs knowing that they have no gift for it, nor ambitions in that direction.'

'How about personal relationships with the other students?'

'Again very male in outlook with a drink or two at the bar, joining in with discussions on current affairs and sport; I just can't imagine her ever having indulged in girlie talk. She clearly had not the slightest interest in clothes or fashion and the idea of her ever having opened a woman's magazine is absurd.'

'How about sex?'

Symonds looked up alertly. 'You would have expected someone like Helen to have been a high libido person, wouldn't you, but there was very little evidence of that in a purely sexual sense. Rumour had it that she had a thing going with Ruth Kendall, but I very much doubt that myself. Ruth was and is a very diffident person and very much lacks self-assurance; she is also very bright and I think Helen just used her as a workmate, someone with whom she could sound out ideas and discuss problems related to their studies. Lots of people here paired up in that way; I did so myself with a fellow who worked at the same sort of pace as I did. Sex has no part in that sort of partnership.

'I think Helen was one of those people for whom sex is just not important. Let me give you an example. The reason I got quite friendly with her was that we used to play squash together quite a bit. At that time, games had already rather fallen apart at St Gregory's, largely because by then the number of female students had overtaken that of the men and a lot of the former competitiveness had become focussed on sex and relationships rather than on the playing fields. Anyway, I was quite good at squash — I played for the university second team, the Squirrels, when I was up at Oxford, and I lacked good opponents here. One day, a few weeks into my first term here, I was waiting to play and watched two of the women from the gallery as they finished their game. It was immediately obvious that Helen was really good; short and compact, she was quick about the court, very fit and had excellent timing. Anyway, I asked her for a game a little later on. It was hard fought and good fun and thereafter we played against each other regularly at squash and also tennis in the summer.

'You asked about sex: something that happened once might give you some idea of what she was like with regard to that. The changing facilities at the squash courts at St Gregory's in those days were pretty primitive to say the least of it. There was only one shower, which led off the changing room, which had a bench with pegs above it on three sides and after playing, the women used to use the facilities in the nurses' hostel in the adjacent block. That day, Helen arrived already changed with her day clothes in a bag and told me that there had been a problem with the plumbing in the hostel and that it was temporarily closed.

'At the end of the game, I expected her to go back to her room, which was only a couple of hundred yards down the road in the open air, but she said: 'I'm sweating like a horse, it's bloody cold out there and I'll share the changing room here with you, if it's all the same to you. Why don't I go first?' With that, she stripped off completely and didn't bother to wrap a towel round herself either then or when she came out of the shower room. I'm quite sure that it wasn't either a come-on, or exhibitionism, it just wasn't an issue with her. When she saw that I had wrapped a towel around my middle, she just went on drying herself as if it was the most natural situation in the world. I can tell you that it wasn't the most natural thing in the world for me.' The man grinned. 'Before you ask, she didn't have a good figure; she was too muscular with not enough up top for most men's taste and certainly mine.

'I liked Helen. She was outspoken to the point of rudeness and was frighteningly clever, but one knew where one was with her.'

'Did you find her aggressive, verbally or physically?'

'Certainly not physically and I never saw her lose her temper, but she could be sarcastic, didn't suffer fools gladly and was prone to put people down, pretty brutally at times, it must be said. She most certainly would never have won a charm contest, but as they say, it takes all sorts.'

'What about Ruth Kendall? You said that she was just about the only friend Helen had.'

'I shouldn't have used the word friend; Ruth was a doormat, a clever and obsessional one, but a doormat none the less, with about as much personality as that utilitarian object. Why did Helen cultivate her? I think it was because she liked to go over and discuss what she had learned with a willing partner and Ruth had the patience and passivity to go along with it. As for Ruth, I'm sure she was lonely and flattered that someone like Helen should have wanted her if not as a friend, a partner at work.'

'So you don't think that she was also a partner of Helen in the other sense of that word?'

'I can't say that I didn't wonder about that, but there was no evidence that I know of to suggest it or any other sexual adventures for either of them. Helen certainly had a high libido, if one uses that term in a broad sense, but in my view that energy was channelled into her work and near-obsessive exercising. She liked running, working out in the gym and in the swimming pool. She certainly had no sexual interest in men; that is, if my experience is anything to go by.'

'Did you ever hear her talk about family matters?'

'Never, but then in my experience it's something that medical students almost never do. Don't ask me why, they just don't. I suppose it's possible that she said something about that to Ruth, but I doubt it somehow.'

'Well, thank you,' Sinclair said. 'You've been most helpful.'

The man nodded. 'It's kind of you to say so. I liked and respected Helen and if I can do anything else to assist you in finding whoever did that terrible thing, you only have to ask.'

★　★　★

Ruth Kendall felt the shiver go right down her spine when Graham Symonds rang her to say that the police would like to talk to her about Helen. She had agreed immediately, somehow knowing that refusal would only have led to at best curiosity and at worst suspicion. At least they were sending down a woman, which might make things easier.

She had the greatest difficulty in concentrating during the afternoon surgery, desperately trying to take her mind off the coming interview, and although she did her best, it didn't mislead one of the patients, a forthright woman who knew her well and had only come for a check on her blood pressure and review of her medication.

'Are you all right?' the woman asked. 'You

don't look yourself at all.'

'I'm just a bit tired.'

'You work too hard,' she said. 'You need a break.'

The woman was right. Things were getting on top of her and while it was true that she did find her job a strain, it wasn't only that; there was the problem of making sure that her three-year-old daughter, Louise, was looked after properly while she was working. In addition to that, there was the recent news of Helen's murder and now a detective was coming to see her.

The pleasant-looking young woman, who arrived punctually later that afternoon, didn't look or sound the least threatening.

'Thank you so much for seeing me so quickly,' she said. 'I was there when Mr Symonds rang you and I know he explained that we are urgently trying to find Helen Vaughan's next of kin. There was nothing in her personal file either at the City Hospital or at St Gregory's and it was the dean, Dr Craxton, who gave us Dr Symonds' name and that's how we got on to you. I gather that Helen was a friend of yours and it would be a great help if you could tell me something about her. You see, it's not only the problem of her next of kin; we are also trying to get as clear a picture of her as we can. We already know about her career and research, but it's personal details that we lack.'

'We did work together as students, but we never discussed that sort of thing — family matters, I mean.'

'Did you keep up with her after you left the hospital?'

'No, I didn't. I never had the time, not with my work and family responsibilities.'

There was a long pause and then the detective smiled at her. 'Is that your little girl?'

Ruth Kendall picked up the framed photograph from the top of the desk, looked at it for a moment and felt her eyes beginning to moisten. 'Yes, it is,' she said, trying desperately to keep the catch out of her voice.

'She's lovely. You and your husband must be very proud of her.'

'I don't have a husband.'

'I'm so sorry. I got the impression from Dr Symonds that you were married.'

Ruth looked away, close to losing control altogether, but the detective's next comment drove all thoughts of self-pity away.

'We have discovered that there was a dark side to Helen's life and we think that that might be related in some way to her death.'

'What do you mean by a dark side?'

'Let me just say that she had a colourful

sex life and if we can find out more about that, it might give us a better chance of finding her killer. So far, you are the only person we have been able to find who had any sort of close relationship with her.'

Ruth felt the beads of perspiration standing out on her forehead and, after a long silence, suddenly made up her mind.

'I'm only going to tell you about her because, whatever her flaws, Helen helped me a great deal when we were students, not least in becoming a far better doctor than I would otherwise have been. Indeed, without her help, I might well not even have finished the course.'

Ruth Kendall was often to wonder in the days and weeks that followed why she had suddenly unburdened herself to the young female detective. It was probably, she thought, that her visit had brought all the memories, which she had fought so hard to bury, flooding back. And there was also the realization that she had been sinking into a deeper and deeper depression and that if she didn't tell someone, she might even end it all.

*   *   *

Ruth Kendall was painfully shy when she arrived at the City Hospital's pre-clinical medical school and she got through the course by the simple expedient of working hard and living quietly in the students' hostel. Almost all the others in her year had only ever used it as a temporary expedient to tide them over until they had made friends and found flats to share with them. Others, with rich parents, even had houses, in which they lived with several others, who paid rent. There were a few long-stay students in the hostel, but the majority were extrovert games-playing men, who were heavily involved in the many extra-curricular student activities. They had no interest at all in the shy, hard-working young woman, who could have been attractive had she had a more outgoing personality and taken more trouble over her appearance. Ruth was not unhappy; she enjoyed the work, applying herself really hard to it, and in her leisure time, listened to music, occasionally went to concerts and films (when she was able to afford it) and took exercise by using the swimming pool. It was in the basement of the nurses' hostel and had been endowed by an ex-matron with the specific condition that it only be used by the nurses and the female medical students and only the latter if they passed muster with the sister tutor. In fact, Ruth was almost the only one who was interested and not many of the nurses used it, either.

Ruth was dreading the start of the clinical course. She knew perfectly well that she wasn't good with people and, being prudish and self-conscious even about her own body, how was she going to be able to cope with those of patients, particularly the male ones? Why hadn't she faced up to that problem right at the beginning of the course? The answer was that she had been pushed towards medicine by an enthusiastic teacher at her school and the ambitions of her parents, who hadn't had much education themselves and saw their clever daughter as a status symbol and a way of enhancing their social standing.

Ruth had had no experience at all of women like Helen Vaughan, who came up to her when the first term of the clinical course was only a week old.

'I've been making enquiries about you,' she said, 'and you're just the person I've been looking for. We're birds of a feather; like me, you're both bright and conscientious, so why don't we work together? I found that tackling problems with work at Cambridge was so much easier if one had someone with whom one could discuss them and ask simple questions, which would have been an embarrassment if put to one of the supervisors. I'm sure you must have experienced that yourself.'

Ruth did hesitate, but not for long. To be asked and, by implication, put in the same bracket as someone like Helen with her double first was a bit daunting, but it was also flattering and it might lead to the support she desperately needed.

Helen had treated her concerns, particularly those related to the examination of patients, robustly, but also with sympathy.

'You must have seen *The Sound of Music* or at least heard the soundtrack.' Ruth nodded. 'And you enjoyed it?' Ruth found herself blushing, not willing to admit to this forthright young woman that not only had she seen it several times on TV, but owned the LP and loved every minute of it, but Helen didn't appear to have noticed. 'Of course you did, so did I and so did many of the people who pour scorn on it. 'I have confidence in confidence alone and I have confidence in me.' Isn't that what Maria sang, or something very like it? Remember that and don't worry, you'll be all right — I'll see to it.'

There was no way that Ruth was able to resist the tsunami of Helen's enthusiasm and the sheer force of her personality and that was how it all began. It started innocuously enough with the two of them measuring each other's blood pressure and making themselves familiar with the use of the auriscope and ophthalmoscope and Ruth was always given the choice of going first or second, but was never allowed to get away with anything.

'Look,' she said one day when Ruth claimed to have seen the optic disc, when she hadn't been able to and was ashamed to admit it, 'never ever tell me, or one of the tutors, that you can understand, see or hear anything that you're not able to, however stupid you may feel about it. I know that lots of the others are doing that all the time, but it's really silly and I promise you that I'll always follow that rule myself. All right?'

'Yes, I'm sorry.'

The first real problem arose when, after having listened to each other's breath sounds through their stethoscopes, Helen said:

'Right, now we're happy with that, it's time for the heart sounds. Off with your bra.' Ruth remembered having blushed scarlet and Helen's brisk response. 'Look,' she said, it's just not possible to listen to the heart sounds, let alone murmurs, through a bra, now is it? I know it's easier for me with all the squash I played at Cambridge where I got used to stripping off completely in the changing room. What's your problem? You're far better up top than I am.' In one swift movement, she unclipped hers and threw it on to a chair. 'Come on. Don't tell me you've forgotten what we've been told already. First, feel for the apex beat with the palm of your hand, assess the cardiac rhythm and then listen over the three sites we've been shown.'

Ruth knew how ridiculous she was being, but when it was Helen's turn, she felt herself blushing and, what made it even worse was that, despite trying to think of something, anything, to take her mind off it and stop it happening, her nipples were standing to attention.

It was after that, Ruth decided to have a chat to Dr Frances Blake. Some years earlier the dean had decided that each student should have access to a member of staff who would be available to them for advice if and when required. Ruth had only met the woman once before, merely to introduce herself and have a brief chat, and had immediately liked her approach, which was friendly and informal, but in no way intrusive.

'What's worrying me,' Ruth said, when she had finally plucked up the courage to see her, 'is that I've been working with another student, with whom I've been having question and answer sessions and we've been using each other as guinea pigs for getting familiar with examination techniques and anything that we haven't understood following lectures and ward rounds. It's been very helpful with many things — I had trouble in locating the optic disc with the ophthalmoscope and my partner encouraged me and was very patient until she was sure I had got it. My worry is what happened yesterday. She suggested that we examine each other's hearts and although I felt uncomfortable about undressing even that far in front of her, she shamed me into doing so, asking me how I could expect to cope with even more intimate examinations of patients unless I had experienced them myself and that I was behaving like a spoilt child, and deserved a sound spanking.

'What she said is true. I am prudish, I hate being seen by others even partly undressed, and it is difficult enough for me to face the idea of even a doctor examining other parts of me, let alone a fellow student. I also felt very uncomfortable using my stethoscope on her; it's not at all the same thing doing it to a patient.'

'You have no problem with that?'

'No, not at all.'

'Is your real worry that the student working with you has a sexual motive behind what she is doing with you?'

Ruth blushed scarlet and nodded. 'I know it's pathetic, but . . . '

'It's not pathetic at all. Remember this: it's

your body and what you do with it is your concern and no one else's. I have no intention of telling you what to do, but it seems to me that you have two choices; either you tell her that you feel uncomfortable about examining each other in any way, but that you value her help and co-operation about the other aspects of your study, or else you dissociate yourself from her completely. I know from our previous brief meeting that you had a sheltered upbringing alone with your mother and there is nothing wrong with you that time and the right experience won't cure. I am here at any time if you should need to talk to me again. All right?'

Ruth had been terrified of facing up to Helen, but she had been working herself up for nothing. The other woman merely shrugged her shoulders and said: 'All right, if that's the way you feel, so be it. You say you want to do general practice. Well, don't blame me if you have trouble coping with the inevitable intimate facets of your work. If you're embarrassed by me, I shudder to think what'll happen if you're faced by a man with piles or prostate problems.'

And so it carried on, both that and the regular question and answer sessions, until they had both qualified, Helen with the prize as the best student of the year and Ruth with honours in medicine from London University. Cambridge didn't make awards in the final medical examinations, but if they had, Ruth was quite sure that Helen would have scooped the pool.

And then, quite suddenly, it was all over. Helen got her first choice of house jobs at the City Hospital and Ruth went to Guildford, thence to a general practice training scheme and finally became a partner in a group there. The ending with Helen had been devastatingly abrupt. Ruth had telephoned her just the once at the City Hospital and the response had been uncompromising, brutally direct and final.

'You should have known better than to ring me when I'm on duty. You're not to do so again, or try to contact me in any other way. Is that quite clear?'

Helen had not even waited for a reply and Ruth was left listening to the dialling tone, the tears running down her cheeks.

★ ★ ★

'Did you ever see her again?'

'No, I didn't, and I did my best to put the whole thing behind me, but it didn't work. Curiously enough, I think it was going to confession some months later that influenced what happened next. I was expecting a serious telling off, but the young priest was sympathetic, which had the effect of making me feel even more sorry for myself. He said that with my sheltered upbringing, despite the fact that I had been in my twenties, it had been nothing more than an adolescent crush, that Helen had taken advantage of me and that I must put it all behind me. He didn't exactly tell me to fulfil myself with a caring husband and a family, but that was the implication.

'It happened at a two-day course that I attended after I had been with the practice for some time. He was working for a pharmaceutical company and I sat next to him at the dinner. He started to flirt with me and we finished up in bed at the hotel. Why did I do it? The alcohol obviously had a bearing on it, he was an attractive person who made me laugh, and underneath it all, I wanted to prove that I was a normal heterosexual woman and what the priest had said was true.'

'And you got pregnant?'

'You've guessed it. How many times have I come across that situation in my practice? 'I was ignorant and didn't really know what I was doing', 'I got carried away', 'I had too much to drink', 'It was an accident — the

116

condom must have had a hole in it', 'I felt all funny at the time and I don't remember what happened and it must have been that date-rape drug'. You must be just as familiar with those stories as I am.

'In my case, the experiment was a hopeless failure. It wasn't that he was rough, or even selfish, and he tried his best to get me to enjoy it, but it didn't work. It didn't hurt, I just felt nothing, and when it was over, he left. I didn't go down to breakfast, we avoided each other for the second day of the conference, and I never saw him again. I could have found out his full name — I only knew him as Brian — but I didn't.

'Why didn't I take the morning-after pill, or have a termination once I knew I was pregnant? It was mainly the Catholic thing, but there was more to it than that; pregnancy, even in the early stages, does strange things to your mind and, hard though it has been in some ways, my daughter has been a great comfort to me and a source of pride, too.'

'What are your feelings about Helen now?'

'There was a time when I hated her for what she had done to me, but then I realized that most of it had been my fault and that faded and I came to recognize that in many ways she had helped me as well. When I heard what had happened to her, there was only sadness at the loss of such a brilliant scientist. She may have been deeply flawed, but who knows why she was like that, or for that matter why any of us are the way we are? Nature, nurture, subtle brain damage at birth, brain-scrambling drugs, or a combination of any of them — believe me, I have thought of all of those with reference to both Helen and myself.

'I am not a fool, nor am I naïve any longer, and I don't believe that you came all the way down here just to get background information about Helen. Graham hinted at or told you about me, didn't he?'

'As a matter of fact, he didn't, just that you knew Helen as well as anyone when you were students together.'

'Well, in view of all I've told you, you no doubt want to know what I was doing the night Helen was killed.'

'It would be helpful.'

'I was at home with Jessica, as I am every night. Our practice does not do night work — that has been contracted out to an emergency service. I'm not entirely comfortable with that arrangement from the patient's point of view, but that's the way it is now and it does make life easier for those in my situation.'

★　★　★

Mark Sinclair had made a bet with himself as to what the doorman of The Blue Elephant Club would look like and smiled with quiet satisfaction at the sight of the bull of a man with the cropped head, broken nose and pock-marked cheeks standing outside.

'Your membership card, sir.'

There was just the amount of stress on the 'sir' to indicate not exactly contempt, but certainly a lack of respect.

'Police,' Sinclair said crisply, showing the man his warrant card. 'I'd like a word with the boss man.'

The doorman nodded, turned to one side and muttered a few words into his pager.

'First door on the left,' he said, standing to one side.

The man who got up from behind the desk looked as if he had modelled himself on a Chicago gangster of the 1920s. He had black hair parted in the middle and so slicked down with oil that it reflected the down-lighters from the ceiling. His black suit, white shirt, multi-coloured tie and the cigar, still with the label on it, completed the picture.

'How can I help you?'

'We're investigating a particularly brutal murder, which occurred last Sunday evening, and we are trying to eliminate as many suspects as possible. This man,' he said, holding out Cahill's photograph, 'claims that he was here between 7 and 10 p.m. on that night. Is there anyone here who might be able to confirm that?'

'Who had you in mind?'

'The doorman, the barman, the bouncer, if you have one, one of the girls, anyone who was on duty that night and who would have seen the punters. I would be quite happy to interview them in your presence; it's a simple matter of identification.'

As Sinclair had hoped, the man visibly relaxed.

'I'll see what I can do, squire.'

When the man had gone, Sinclair glanced up at the bank of TV monitors mounted high on the wall opposite the desk. The pictures weren't all that clear, but he could make out a red-haired girl doing a pole dance without any great show of enthusiasm and only two of the lap-dancing bays were occupied, neither girl matching the description that Cahill had given him.

In the event, none of the men or women who came into the room was either able or willing to identify Cahill from the photograph, but Sinclair was almost certain that the one in question was the third girl. She had roughly the right build and hair colouring and seemed to him to be the most nervous, a tiny muscle in her left eyelid continuously flickering. He had deliberately timed his arrival to be within twenty minutes of the change of shift that Cahill had told him about and after he had thanked the man in charge, left the club and waited across the street within sight of both the main and side exits, the latter opening on to a narrow passageway. The girl in question came out a few minutes after ten and once he had established that there was no one with or following her, he hurried after her, catching up a hundred or so yards short of the entrance to the underground station.

She turned, all the colour draining out of her face, when he called out the name that Cahill had given him and she saw who it was.

'I just want a quick word with you. There's a café over there — why don't we have a cup of tea or a coffee?'

He saw the look of panic on her face and for a moment thought she was going to make a run for it, but then her shoulders dropped.

'We could always go to Canon Row if you'd prefer it and one of the WPCs could always check that your rather fancy hairstyle of you know where tallies with the description that that man gave us.'

Sinclair hated himself for treating her like that, but he had an instinct that if he had not done so she would probably have continued to deny any knowledge of Cahill.

'All right.'

'Look,' he said when they were sitting opposite each other, 'you probably think it's unfair my bullying you like that, but a young woman, not a great deal older than you, was brutally murdered last Sunday evening, some time between seven and midnight. This man,' he said, pulling out Cahill's photograph again, 'says he was in the club roughly between seven and ten, then went with you to the Rushton Hotel until roughly 11.45. All I need to know is if that is true.'

After looking straight at him for a few moments, the young woman said: 'All right, he had a drink or two while watching the pole dancers, I did my act for him and yes, we went to the hotel together after my stint was over, soon after ten.'

'What outdoor clothes were you wearing when you did that?'

'Why do you need to know that?'

'Because I have to check with the porter at the hotel.' He nodded when she told him. 'Have you been with him before?'

'Yes.'

'Has he ever in any sense been violent to you?'

'No. He wanted me to do certain things

that are unacceptable to me, but he took my refusal without making too much of it. Mostly he just wanted to talk. It was the usual thing; his wife didn't understand him, she was cold and didn't like it. Tony won't have to be told about this, will he?'

'Who, the bloke in the office?'

'Yes.'

'Not if you've told me the truth.'

'I have.'

Sinclair nodded. 'I'm very grateful for your help. Look after yourself.'

For the first time, a flicker of a smile crossed her face. 'Don't worry, I will.'

Sinclair knew perfectly well that he ought to have got the girl's address and even arranged an identity parade, but there was the fact that she had provided Cahill with an adequate alibi and also that he didn't believe the man could possibly have killed Helen Vaughan. The event had been far too calculated for an obviously impulsive man like him and, without enquiring, how could he have known where the pathology department was in the hospital, let alone have been able to get in once there? It wasn't only that — in a thoroughly unprofessional way, he felt sorry for the girl having to make a living in the way she did. There were some of his colleagues who would have taken a positive delight in bullying her, even to the extent of demanding a freebie, a thought that he found even more depressing. There were those who claimed that quite a few of the girls enjoyed selling themselves, some being students and others moonlighting from jobs such as nursing, but even if that were true, he still found it sad.

Despite being so disillusioned by the whole sordid business, Sinclair knew that he had to check at the hotel and went there before he weakened and changed his mind. He strongly suspected that the man on the desk was an illegal immigrant and his task wasn't made any easier by the language difficulty. In the end, though, he was satisfied that the man had recognized Cahill's photograph and he was also able to give an adequate description of the girl and the clothes she had been wearing.

7

'Well, Cahill's in the clear,' Sinclair said as he sat opposite Sarah as the train pulled out of Liverpool Street Station early the following afternoon. He put his notebook on the table top between them and consulted it at intervals as he told her what he had done the previous evening. 'The man is as odious a specimen as I have met in a long time, but his alibi from seven to midnight on that Sunday is pretty solid and I think we can rule him out.'

'How about Symonds? What did he have to say?'

'He did confirm what we already knew and that was that Helen Vaughan was very much on the masculine side of the male/female continuum with a liking for detail and being very competitive both at work and in the games of tennis and squash they played together. There appeared to be no room for emotion and not much milk of human kindness, either. And what about Ruth Kendall?'

Sarah gave him a detailed account of her meeting with the GP. 'If her account is to be believed, Helen discarded her with hardly a thought as soon as she was no longer of any use to her either at work or at play, if I can put it that way. The end of their relationship was terminated quite suddenly and brutally and I couldn't help thinking that another suicide was only very narrowly avoided.'

'Did you believe her?'

'In essence, yes, but I suspect that the sex bits weren't quite so limited as she implied, nor was she as much the innocent victim as she made out. I'm quite certain, though, that she had nothing to do with Helen's murder.'

'How about the sado-masochistic stuff that Helen seemed so attached to?'

'There was just one episode in which Ruth Kendall claimed that she was threatened with a spanking, but I have a shrewd suspicion that it might have been carried out.'

Mark raised his eyebrows and Sarah grinned back at him as she described the circumstances.

'Nothing on any relatives or family background?'

'Not a thing, I'm afraid.'

'Well, let's hope we get something out of today. So far we just seem to have been treading water.'

'Ancient seats of learning aren't exactly my patch,' Sarah said, 'not that I have anything against them, but knowing that you're familiar with the environment, I'm sure you'd make a much better job of tackling the man in question. Will you take the interview on?'

'All right, but I'm not so sure about the better job bit. You have a very persuasive way about you.'

Within two hours of leaving London, they were sipping cups of tea in Dr Rowson's rooms. The senior tutor was a great bear of a man, almost completely bald and wearing a rumpled suit, but there was nothing threatening about his manner — rather the reverse — and his expression was both benign and alert.

'I was really shocked when I heard about Helen Vaughan's death,' he said. 'I can't claim to have known her really well, but this is a friendly college and I take an interest in all the students. I also have details of her academic record here, which was truly outstanding, and she is a tremendous loss to medicine and science. You can't ask for much more than an entry scholarship, a first in both parts of the natural sciences tripos and a couple of college prizes. She was offered a research fellowship here, but chose to qualify in medicine first. She certainly knew her mind, that young woman.'

'How about extra-curricular activities?'

'She was a good squash player, captain of the college women's team, and was also in the tennis side, but the medical students are kept pretty hard at it, you know, what with dissection and practicals in physiology and she didn't have much spare time.'

'Any special friends amongst the other students?'

'There was one young woman she was very close to, who was also in the squash side, as I recall, and I'm sure that our archivist would be able to find her name and even a photograph of the team as it won the 'cuppers' competition in their final year.'

'Do you by any chance have a record of her next of kin?'

'Yes, I do. It was a Professor Warnfield; he was head of the department of physiology at Oxford, Helen's uncle, and one of my closest friends here when we were undergraduates together.'

'You said 'was' on a couple of occasions.'

'Yes, he died of stomach cancer about three years ago. He was only fifty-five and a great loss in his field.'

'Do you know if he was married, or had any other relatives we might contact?'

'I have a copy of his obituary here and it finishes by stating: 'Henry Warnfield never married.' '

'How come that obituary got into Helen Vaughan's file?'

'It didn't. I got a copy from our archivist when I knew that you were coming.' There was a very long pause while the man fiddled with the papers. 'There is one other thing, which I promised both Professor Warnfield and Helen Vaughan that I wouldn't disclose, but as both of them have died and Helen under such appalling circumstances, I feel that it is my duty to tell you about it. You see, when the two of them came up here for her interview, Warnfield asked me to see him on his own and told me that Helen had just changed her name from Charlotte Dickinson to Helen Vaughan by deed poll and that she did not want anyone to know about it, not even the rest of her family or the school.

'I remember saying that I didn't see how that would be possible. After all, apart from her exam results, she had had glowing references from her school and we would have to let them know if she was successful in her application — she might even get an entry scholarship if she interviewed well and excelled in the special paper we set our candidates. He took the point, but said that a letter to the school saying that Charlotte Dickinson, although having great potential, was rather immature and would benefit from a year off doing some voluntary work, perhaps overseas, would be in her best interests, perhaps before reapplying.

'My immediate reaction was that doing such a thing was out of the question, but then he told me his reasons for asking were to do with the family and when I still demurred, he went on to say exactly what they were and if they became public knowledge, the consequences for Helen would be dire and he didn't even rule out suicide. Furthermore, he made me swear a solemn oath never to divulge this information to anyone else.'

The man looked straight at Sinclair and nodded. 'I know what you're thinking and that is that now that the two of them are both dead and that as a murder has been committed, my promise no longer has any meaning. May I just say this? I have already given you her birth name and I will extend that to that of her school, a copy of the details of her academic and extra-curricular activities here and that photograph I mentioned, and if your further enquiries fail to bear fruit I will be prepared to break my vow about the rest of it.'

Sinclair didn't hesitate. 'You can't say fairer than that,' he said. The man's relief and surprise were obvious and the detective also noticed Sarah's quizzical expression. 'I'll let you know how we get on.'

*   *   *

It was a few minutes before five when the two detectives left the college and began to walk along King's Parade towards the station.

'Now that I think about it, I'm sure you took exactly the right line with that Rowson fellow,' Sarah said. 'I'm quite sure that doing a bully-boy act wouldn't have worked, but what on earth do you suppose the sinister family secret is?'

'We'll just have to hope that something comes out of a visit to Branscombe College. I suggest we go tomorrow. The name mean anything to you, Sarah?'

'No, never heard of it.'

'Neither have I, but I know the area around Oxford pretty well and the village mentioned in the address is no more than ten miles from the city centre. I think a visit there after we've seen Tyrrell tomorrow morning would be a good idea. In the meantime, I think a little recreation might be in order.'

Sarah looked across at him, feeling herself flush and the sinking feeling deep in the pit of her stomach. If he meant by a little recreation what she thought he meant, where were they going to go? A hotel? She just knew that that wouldn't be right; it had sleazy, rather sordid connotations in her mind.

'Ever been punting?'

'No.'

'It's fun and you must have a go.'

Sarah gave him a warm smile, all her tension suddenly evaporating, realizing that she had just got carried away and that her idea had been utterly ridiculous.

'Why don't we go up towards Grantchester?' Sinclair said, when they had climbed into the punt. 'If, as I suspect, we make fools of ourselves, I'd rather we did it in peace and quiet rather than in front of everyone in the colleges.'

One thing was very clear, Sarah thought, and that was that there was no question of Mark making a fool of himself. He stood, perfectly balanced on the platform at the stern of the punt, dropped the pole in vertically and pushed, sending them straight and surprisingly quickly upstream.

'Now it's your turn.'

Sarah didn't hesitate, followed his instructions and, first standing in the body of the punt, got used to handling the pole and trying some tentative pushes. After ten minutes or so, she had the confidence to climb on to the stern platform and managed to get them moving in a reasonably straight line.

'Well done,' he said, 'that was terrific for a first time. Why not leave it at that, otherwise I guarantee that you'll be as stiff as a board tomorrow.'

Sarah lay back on the cushions and when, a minute or two later, he steered the punt to the bank where there was an overhanging willow and settled down beside her, covering them with her coat, it was only too obvious that there was something else just as stiff.

The 'little recreation' proved to be every bit as exciting as her earlier imaginings. There was the tension as he turned her on to her side facing the river, the effort of trying to pretend to the people in the passing punts, whom she could see through half-closed eyes, that they were just having a snooze, and the almost unbelievable pleasure as he slipped smoothly inside her and the final explosion of sensation when she lost herself completely.

She slowly returned to full consciousness to the accompaniment of the gentle movement of a finger on her cheek.

'Sarah, are you awake?'

She let out an almost inaudible sigh. 'Just about.'

'There's something I need to tell you. You see, when I was a student at Oxford, I met a girl who was doing the same modern languages course as me and we hit it off straightaway. In many ways, it was an attraction of opposites: she was fun and I was a bit dour, she was like quicksilver intellectually and I was a mere plodder and as to bed . . . Well, let me put it this way, she liked the spice and pickle and I was a touch inhibited, to say the least of it.

'We got married soon after we obtained our degrees. She got a job in a publishing house, I started in one of the big travel agencies and we were so happy together. It happened when we were on holiday in Majorca about a year later. We had had a swim and were sunbathing on the beach just below our hotel, when she gave me one of her special looks and back we went to our room. She was kneeling astride me on the bed, looking down with the expression on her face that I had got to know so well, when she suddenly let out an agonized cry, just had time to put her hand to her head and then fell sideways. She died at that moment, Sarah. She'd had a fatal subarachnoid haemorrhage.

'The doctors, my mother, my friends and, most of all, my in-laws, who were wonderful, all told me the same things. It was nobody's fault, least of all mine, it could not have been predicted and I must try to put it behind me.

I knew perfectly well that what they were saying made sense, but it was one thing to acknowledge that and quite another to put it out of my mind. Every time I met an attractive girl, all the memories returned and I backed away.

'As a result I hid myself away from my old friends, left my job, joined the police, got accelerated promotion and before coming here, I worked with the Thames Valley people. Why did I move from there? Well, I worked with a WPC for a time and she was just the wrong person for me, full of childhood traumas and neuroses and like a fool, I must have encouraged her in some way, because she became something of a clinging vine.

'Why didn't I back away from you the other night, then? It was because of the way you are. We got on so well together right from the start, you were fun to be with and, don't be embarrassed, there was also your reaction to those tapes.' He turned towards her and smiled. 'It was just the same for me. I have never had the slightest impulse to hurt anyone, or be hurt, but that wasn't the point of those tapes, was it? Those two people were really getting a kick out of what they were doing and they were really enjoying it and, let's be honest, so were we watching it. I have to admit that I might well have hesitated when we went into your flat, but then you took command and I promise you my previous problem never entered my head, entirely thanks to you.'

Sarah turned her head slowly to look at his concerned face.

'I should have told you before, but the time never seemed right.'

'I'm so sorry,' she said, near to tears, her voice cracking slightly. 'It was very brave of you to tell me and I'm so glad you did. I can't think of the right words now, but I want you to know that whatever should happen between us, I would never want or expect you to try to forget that you loved your wife very much nor the wonderful times you must have had together.'

*   *   *

'You both did an excellent job yesterday,' Tyrrell said, when his two assistants had given him an account of their enquiries at the two hospitals and Helen Vaughan's college at Cambridge, 'and I agree that you should visit Branscombe College right away. I haven't heard of it, either, so let's see what we can dig up on the Internet.'

The college did have a website and it proved to be a large, single-sex day school.

There were details of its history, the number of pupils, organization, fees and the names of the headmistress and those on its board of governors.

'I believe that there's no substitute for personal contact in a situation like this,' Tyrrell said, 'so I'll give the place a ring right away and pressure them to give you both an appointment with the headmistress as soon as you can get there.'

The college was set in large grounds and it looked as if the main building had, at one time, been a country house, but that had been almost completely swallowed up by extensions and new blocks in a variety of styles.

'What I know about private single-sex girls' schools could easily be written on an economy label,' Sinclair said as they pulled up outside the main entrance, 'and I'm quite sure that you'll be able to get far more out of the teachers than I ever would. Why don't you handle the interview with the head?'

'All right, but I assure you that a place like this is every bit as alien to me.'

Miss Agnew proved to be a slim, elegant woman, who, Sarah thought, could not have been more than in her middle forties at most.

'I'm very sorry to hear about this young woman, Charlotte Dickinson,' the woman said after the detective had explained that her death had been quite unexpected and that they were trying to trace her next of kin.

'Let's see, now, roughly what years are we talking about?'

'She was born in 1969, so I suppose she would have come here in the early eighties or thereabouts.'

'Well, that was long before my time here; the person you need is Muriel Wishart. She taught history for many years here and is now our archivist and she also helps in the library.'

'Is she likely to be in today?'

The woman smiled. 'Oh yes, this place has been her life for more than forty years and she's in every day. She's also writing a history of the college, which is due to be published to coincide with our centenary in a couple of years' time.'

'She won't mind our interrupting her labours, I hope?'

'She'll welcome it, if I know Muriel. I'll give her a ring right away and my secretary will take you to her.'

Muriel Wishart was a large, untidy woman with a booming voice and a ready laugh, which made her jowls wobble and Sinclair was irresistibly reminded of Margaret Rutherford as Madame Arcati in the film of Nöel Coward's *Blythe Spirit*, of which he had seen a new theatre production in the West End only a few weeks earlier.

'Charlotte Dickinson, you said, born on 12 June 1969, which means in the normal course of events she would have come here at the start of the winter term of 1982. How awful that she should have died so young; you see, I remember her well.'

'You do? I'm most impressed.'

'Well, not many of the girls here are as bright as she was and I can't think why Cambridge wanted her to take a gap year, particularly as she does not appear to have taken it up. Terrible waste, that. I was her form mistress for a year and someone like her sticks in the memory, I can tell you.'

The woman switched on her laptop and opened a file, then began scrolling down.

'Ah, here we are. Marvels of modern science, eh? You'd think that an old buffer like me wouldn't be able to tolerate a thing like this, let alone know how to use it, and would still be working on parchment with a quill pen, wouldn't you? Well, you'd be wrong — took to it like a duck to water. Wizard piece of technology!'

'It must have been some task getting all your records on to it, though.'

'It was and I have to confess that I needed help with scanning the old photographs and getting 'em all in the right place. Keeping up to date's a doddle, though.'

Sarah, who was trying, without much success, to keep a straight face, blushed as the woman suddenly looked at her, then let out a loud guffaw.

'Don't worry, m'dear, your self-control is admirable; you should see the girls' reaction to my 1940s speak, they fall apart. Let's see now.' The woman squinted at the screen. 'Charlotte arrived here as a day girl in the autumn of 1982. Previously, she had been at a mixed prep school, which was owned and run by her father, and she also lived at the same address.'

'Do you know if her parents are still alive?'

'Her father certainly isn't. He died in the late eighties and his school closed down — I believe there had been financial problems for some time before that.'

'Did you ever meet either of her parents?'

'Only her mother. I remember having a discussion with her about Charlotte's options for a university place — I gathered that Mr Dickinson was already unwell at the time. Cambridge came up because Mrs Dickinson's brother had been there and she decided to give it a try. In those days having a relative at a place like that counted for something and that was no bad thing, if you want my opinion. Social inclusion is all very well, but it can be carried too far. Do you know, some colleges at Oxbridge have even had to appoint tutors to teach new arrivals basic English! Talk about dumbing down!'

'What was the girl like?'

'Very forthright and rather aggressive when she first came here, which I suppose might have been due to her having been at that particular preparatory school. You see, quite a few of the boys were boarders, but none of the girls except for Charlotte. She lived with her parents in the private accommodation, of course, but inevitably must have had contact with the boys, for example at weekends, in a way that the other girls at that school never did.'

'Was she popular here?'

'It is certainly possible to be popular even if you are good at everything, as Charlotte was, but not if you parade it. False modesty was not part of her make-up, but she did mellow quite a bit as she got older and particularly following her illness.'

'Illness? What was that?'

The woman scrolled down to the next page. 'I see that it started towards the end of 1984. I don't know the details, but she was off for the whole of the spring term of 1985. The doctor's certificate stated that she had

had glandular fever with complications, but there are no further details recorded here.'

'Is there a photograph of her by any chance?'

'Yes, there is.'

Miss Wishart brought it up on the screen and, looking over her shoulder, the two detectives saw a girl with shoulder-length, very fair hair looking straight at the camera.

'What astonishing eyes!'

'Yes. I was struck by them myself and asked her about it as her mother had light brown ones. She told me that they were just like her father's; I remember that because it was the only time she so much as mentioned him.'

'Not a great one for smiling, I imagine.'

'You're quite right; she was driven, directional and frighteningly clever. Making jokes or having close friends was most definitely not part of her agenda.'

'Well, thank you very much. Perhaps I might have the address of where her father's school used to be; there might be someone living close by who knows where Mrs Dickinson is living now.'

'This might also be of some help,' the woman said, and Sinclair did not fail to notice the hint of a smile on her face as she brought the index back on to the screen. 'You see, Charlotte had a much younger sister,

142

who was here from 1998 to 2001.'

The woman clicked the mouse and moved the cursor, bringing up another picture on the screen. 'Ah, here we are. Emily Jane Dickinson, born 15 March 1985. As you see, she was very like her sister, with the same fair hair and blue eyes, but she lacked her intensity and focus. There is no doubt that she was also intellectually gifted, but without Charlotte's drive.'

'She wasn't here very long.'

'No, her mother was asked to take her away in the summer of 2001, when she was sixteen, although she was allowed to take her GCSEs. She was supervised individually — Miss Hudson, who was head at that time and one of the old school, didn't want to run the risk of contaminating the other girls.'

'Drugs?'

'How did you guess? It was only cannabis, but we have a zero-tolerance rule here.'

'I'm surprised that the name Dickinson didn't immediately ring a bell with Miss Agnew, even if she wasn't head at that time. It must have been somewhat of a cause célèbre; I don't suppose all that many girls here are expelled,' Sinclair said.

'That particular bell is disconnected in her case. She's only the administrative head, really, mainly involved with finance, fund-raising, dealing with staff and policy matters, while Mrs Cranfield is the person who is in charge of the academic and pastoral side, if one likes to put it that way.'

The woman raised her eyebrows and turned her eyes back to the computer screen.

'Do you happen to know Mrs Dickinson's current address?' Sarah asked.

The woman clicked the mouse and scrolled down again.

'Ah, here we are, Mrs Patricia Dickinson. There is an address and phone number here and I imagine it's the place she moved to after the school closed, but there's no guarantee that she's still there, of course. I'll jot down the details for you, if you like.'

'Thank you.'

'Oh, Inspector . . . '

'Yes.'

'There's a story behind Charlotte's death, isn't there?'

'What makes you think that?'

'Well, I can't be expected to believe that not one but two police inspectors would come all this way if there wasn't one, now can I?'

Sarah smiled. 'No comment is what is usually said in circumstances like these and I suppose it serves as well as anything else.'

'I didn't think either of you'd tell me, but if

one doesn't ask, one never learns, does one?'

'Was that one of your dicta when you were teaching?' Sinclair asked.

Miss Wishart let out a loud chuckle, which set her jowls in motion. 'Advantage server, I'd say. You can use the extension through there, should you wish to give her a call,' she said, pointing to the inner door. 'Let me hasten to assure you that I won't listen in.'

'Of course you wouldn't, but then it wouldn't be fair to expose you to the temptation, would it? My colleague here will, I'm quite sure, be only too happy to keep you company.'

The woman threw up her hands. 'Game, set and match.'

She waited until Sinclair had left the room, closing the door behind himself.

'Not many flies on your colleague, are there? Good-looking fellow, too!'

Sarah couldn't immediately think of a reply to either comment and contented herself with giving the woman a smile.

★   ★   ★

'I imagine you didn't tell Mrs Dickinson that her daughter was dead?' Sarah said as they drove into the village of Tubney, just outside Oxford.

'No, I didn't.'

'I wouldn't have done so, either. It was one of the things that Tyrrell taught me when I first started to work with him as a DC. I remember his saying that most people guess that there's bad news coming under circumstances like this, but one often learns things by watching their reactions to it and occasionally they'll even faint, so the telephone is not a good idea, nor is it wise to tell people if you're on your own.'

'I wish someone had done the same thing for me; I remember only too well the terrible mess I made of it the first time round.'

The house was small and semi-detached and was in a crescent. All the buildings there were of similar design and it looked as if the whole development had been put up at the same time.

'It's about Emily, isn't it?' the woman asked when they were sitting in the living room.

'No, Charlotte, I'm afraid,' said Sarah. 'You see, she died last Sunday. We would of course have told you earlier, but we had great difficulty in finding you.'

'Oh, my God!'

For one moment, Sinclair thought that the woman was going to faint and mimed the sipping of a cup of tea as he made his way towards the kitchen. Sarah went across to where the woman was sitting and put her arm round her shoulders.

'I'm so sorry to have had to break the news so abruptly, but I thought that it would have been even worse had we done so over the phone.'

The woman looked up, the colour already beginning to come back into her face.

'It's all right, you couldn't help it. What happened to her?'

'There's no way I can break this to you gently, either. She was killed in her laboratory. The one consolation is that it happened abruptly and she wouldn't have suffered.'

'Killed, you say? Not the professor who was murdered in her office at the City Hospital? I saw it on the news on TV last night.'

'So the name Helen Vaughan didn't mean anything to you?'

The woman shook her head miserably. 'How did you find out about me?'

Sarah explained how they had been to both medical schools and her college at Cambridge and how that had led to Branscombe School.

Not for the first time, Sarah marvelled at the way the tea seemed to work as the woman relaxed a little and began to tell them about her daughter.

Patricia Warnfield was just eighteen when she went to work at Farley Grange Preparatory School in 1965 as under-matron. James Dickinson was just too young to have served in the war and after National Service from 1947 to 1949, he went up to Oxford, leaving with a first-class degree in classics. His father had owned and run the school since the late 1920s and was delighted when his only child agreed at first to teach there and then to take it over completely five years later.

Under James Dickinson's direction the school flourished, the number of pupils increased, a new wing was built and, in the late sixties, day girls were introduced. The fees were considerable but the facilities were good, the food excellent and the number of scholarships and exhibitions to leading public schools steadily increased.

Patricia admired Dickinson, she enjoyed the work and when, two years later, the matron retired and he asked her to take over the position, she was both flattered and glad to do so. She had known right from the start that James was a strict disciplinarian and was a devotee of corporal punishment — could she have failed to notice the visible evidence of it when the boarders were taking their baths and showers. She was well aware, too, that it was common enough in prep schools at that time and the boys never seemed the worse for it.

It was at the beginning of the summer term, when she had been matron since the previous September, that James Dickinson asked her to marry him. It was strange, she was to think years later, that she should have agreed with almost no hesitation. James was extremely clever, widely read in many fields and took delight in sharing his expertise with her right from the time she had first gone to the school, giving her books to read and making sense of the more difficult ones with his gift for rendering complex ideas into simple language.

'You're really very bright, you know,' he said to her one day, 'and it's such a pity that you never went to university, but we can easily make up for that together.'

It hadn't been that Patricia's parents had been against higher education for girls, it was just that both had died in a sailing accident when she was just eighteen. Her brother, who was a real high flier and had just come down from Cambridge, wasn't earning all that much at the time and they both discovered that their parents seeming affluence was largely an illusion. Their house was heavily mortgaged, there were other loans, and had it not been for their life insurance policies, the debts would never have been paid.

Academic subjects were not the only things that James taught her. He knew all about sex, too, things that she had not heard about, and introduced them gradually into their love life, taking it slowly, giving her a taste for it before marriage, and the rest followed with her enthusiastic cooperation.

The first cloud on the horizon appeared not when she was pregnant, but when the boy, whom James was quite convinced they were going to have, turned out to be a girl. If Patricia had been older and more sophisticated, she would probably have realized much earlier that her husband was in denial and that, in his eyes, their child was a boy. Their particular circumstances also fed his obsession. There were girls at the school by then, but none of them was a boarder, so Charlotte, whom James invariably called Charlie, played with the boys and took part in their rough and tumbles.

It was when Charlotte was about ten years old having a bath that Patricia saw the three horizontal, parallel, purple lines on her bottom.

'Did your father do that?'

The girl had traced the slightly raised

ridges with her forefinger and grinned.

'Peak, Berry and I were fooling around near the cricket pavilion on Sunday and we broke one of the windows. He caned all three of us. I didn't mind — we deserved it and I wouldn't have wanted him to treat me any differently from the others.'

Patricia didn't like it, but Charlotte obviously didn't bear her father any resentment and she had an instinct that if she spoke to James about it, it would only make things harder for the girl. She was to think later that the fact that she had stopped going into the bathroom when Charlotte was in there was, in a sense, burying her head in the sand — but the girl was beginning to want her privacy. Had that sort of punishment stopped when Charlotte went to Branscombe College? Patricia convinced herself that it had, not least because the girl's periods had started at about that time.

Patricia's greatest regret in the years following Charlotte's birth was that despite being investigated by a gynaecologist and trying every piece of advice, sensible or crazy, that she had gleaned from women's magazines, she failed to get pregnant again and James's attitude, implying that it was all her fault, only made it worse.

It was early in 1983 that her world fell

apart. The door to Charlotte's bedroom had been left a few inches open and as she walked past it, she looked through the gap. The girl was standing in front of the full-length mirror in just her bra and pants, gently massaging her stomach, and that glance was enough to see that Charlotte was pregnant. She turned away, somehow knowing that to tackle her there and then without careful thought might well make matters worse than they were already. The significance of the little glances between father and daughter, his hand that used to rest just too long around her shoulders — which Patricia had told herself was just his way of showing harmless affection and which she had tried to ignore — was now only too obvious and she had not the slightest doubt that James was responsible. Once the painful talk she had had with Charlotte confirmed her worst fears and that the girl hadn't told anyone about it, not even James, the really serious thought began.

A week later, she knocked loudly on the door of her husband's study and walked in without waiting for a response. He was sitting behind his desk with a magazine in front of him and in one swift movement, he put it into the central drawer, locked it and slipped the key into the pocket of his jacket.

'Patricia, this is too much, you know — '

'Shut up, James, and listen carefully to what I have to say. Charlotte is pregnant and we both know who was responsible.'

He looked at her with an expression that she was to think later was almost one of triumph. 'If you're thinking of getting rid of my son — '

'I told you to shut up!' she shouted, desperate to stop him saying anything further. Taking off her shoe, she brought it down on the top of the desk so hard that the heel gouged a piece of wood out of the surface. 'One more word from you, just one more syllable, and I'll go straight to the police. I am the one who is pregnant and Charlotte has just gone down with a severe attack of glandular fever, which means that she will have to miss the whole of next term at Branscombe. I don't propose to tell you where we are going, but when we come back — I hope and expect at the end of March — Charlotte will be able to go back to the college for the summer term and you and I will have the second child we've both been hoping for. As for you, you'll never so much as touch Charlotte again. Should you choose to make difficulties, any difficulties at all, you will certainly be ruined and probably be sent to prison. Denying paternity or refusing to cooperate with the birth certification won't do you any good either. I don't know whether or not you keep up with the latest medical research, but recent work on DNA rules out any uncertainty in these matters.'

★ ★ ★

'How did it all work out?' Sinclair asked.

'It did and it didn't. I realized later what appalling risks I had taken over the birth itself, but it all went quite easily and beforehand, I had the time to do some research into it and even managed to persuade one of the obstetricians at a hospital near to where I had rented a flat to let me watch some normal deliveries. I claimed to be writing a novel and that I wanted some authentic background. I discovered that fifteen was by no means a bad time to have a first baby and when the time came I knew exactly what to do and there were no problems. Naturally I had anxieties about possible complications, but there were none.

'The biggest mistake I made was to believe that I would be able to go back to the school with Charlotte and the baby and that all would be well. It wasn't. Charlotte wouldn't eat, James wouldn't speak to either of us, and I was still trying to get used to managing a tiny baby again and the formula bottle feeding that I had instituted right from the beginning — breast feeding was out of the question, not only because Charlotte would be returning to school but also because I was worried that it might have created bonding difficulties for her.

'It was my brother John who saved the day. He was already in a senior position as reader in physiology at Oxford with a good chance of becoming professor and head of the department in the future and on the first weekend after our return I went to see him. He immediately offered to have Charlotte to live with him until the dust had really settled. John had a medical degree and had done sufficient clinical work to become a registered practitioner before he moved to physiology. He was the first person I had told about Charlotte's baby and had been the one to supply the medical certificate for the school. She had always been fond of him; he treated her as a gifted young woman rather than as a tiresome adolescent, listening to and discussing her ideas and opinions with her. John was a bachelor and remained one until he so sadly died, but he had a biggish house and had a live-in housekeeper, who was an uncomplicated and motherly soul, whom Charlotte also liked.

'This arrangement meant that I had to do a

lot of driving, John's house being some twenty miles from Branscombe, but much more disturbing for me, though, was that Charlotte began to speak to me less and less and finally ignored me completely. 'Don't worry,' John said to me one day, 'she'll come round to you in due course.' He was wrong, she never did, and after I had picked her up after her last day at school, I never saw her again.

'Of course, John kept me in touch with how she was doing at Cambridge and we agreed that pressing her to see me would be counter-productive. The final blow came when he and I had a long talk just before she left university and it must have been as difficult for him as it was for me. 'What I have to tell you is going to be very hurtful,' he said, 'and, believe me, I have thought long and hard about it. The fact is that in my judgement, Charlotte is going to make a major contribution to science and, equally, I don't believe that there is any hope of her being reconciled to you in the short term. It's not that she blames you in any way for what happened; it is true that there was a time when she did, feeling that you ought to have realized what was going on and protected her from it, but as she got older and more mature, she came to understand that that was unfair and that immediately you had discovered it, you did everything possible to shield her from the worst consequences of her father's actions. She is convinced, though, that the only way for her to move forward is for everyone to accept the status quo and forget what happened — she has even gone as far as to change her name.' '

'And so you never did see her again?' Sinclair said.

'No, nor did I find out if John's prediction about her future was correct, and although I read about Professor Vaughan's career in the paper the other day, it never occurred to me that she might be Charlotte. It is, though, a great consolation to know that despite everything, my daughter did achieve great success and made real advances in her field.'

'There is no doubt about that,' said Sarah. 'Have you any idea who killed her, or why?'

'Not yet, but we are doing everything possible to find out who did. How about Emily? How did she get on?' The woman let out a deep sigh and Sarah immediately held up her hand. 'Don't worry if you feel you've had enough — we can always come back. It's just that we didn't want to approach her without checking with you first.'

'It's all right. You see, I don't know where she is and I would like to explain why.'

As far as the new baby was concerned, for the next fifteen years the outcome exceeded Patricia's greatest expectations. To start with, James took not the slightest notice of her, but to her surprise that gradually changed. Patricia drew the line at letting Emily attend James's school and never once did she let him be alone with her, but when she was about six, he started to teach her simple card games, which led to jigsaws, draughts and chess. As well as his ability with classics, James also had a talent for modern languages, and he lavished a great deal of time in helping her with French and German once she had started them at school.

It was when Emily was twelve that James first became ill with the lymphoma that was to kill him three years later. There could be no denying that by then Emily had grown to love her father deeply and she became more and more distressed as he steadily became weaker. Patricia still wouldn't let her go into his room without being close by herself and it must have been only about two weeks before he died that Emily had been playing Scrabble with him in his bedroom and she was doing some ironing in the adjacent dressing room with the communicating door open. She had her back to them and could hear them chatting, but was unable to pick out any of the words, when quite suddenly the girl let out an eerie wail and, deathly pale, ran past into the corridor and locked herself in the bathroom.

James was lying against the pillows, gaunt and his complexion grey, and refused to answer her questions. After that, it was one thing after another. James died only two weeks later, Emily refused to speak to her other than in monosyllables, and then there was the shock of discovering that James had willed everything to the two girls and that she had been left out altogether.

*   *   *

'The only explanation I can think of for what happened is that James must have told her who her birth mother was, but I never did discover the truth; James hardly said a word to me in the two weeks left before he died and Emily was both rude and uncooperative. She refused to go to James's funeral even though I tried to explain that he had done his best to be a good father to her and that I knew she had loved him, but that only provoked a torrent of abuse.'

'You mentioned the will. How was that resolved?'

'With difficulty and once again it was John who did all the background work. There was the problem that I had been left out of it completely, which was one of the first things that had to be sorted out, that of contacting Charlotte (John was the only person who knew where she was), that of the sale of the school and house in which we lived, and that of Emily, who wasn't of age. The final upshot, after endless meetings with lawyers, was that I received enough to buy this place and just about enough income to live on. The fact that I am now comfortably off is due to the one thing that has upset me more than anything else. You see, unbeknown to me, John had been suffering from cancer for some time and he died about a year later, leaving me enough money to live comfortably. As far as the rest of James's money was concerned, which was more than I had expected, that was left in equal shares to Charlotte and Emily. It is some consolation to know that Charlotte made a success of her life.'

'What an absolute nightmare all of it must have been for you.'

'It was.'

'And how about Emily? What happened to her?'

'That was the most distressing thing of all, even more than John's death. Her behaviour became worse and worse. She was caught smoking cannabis at school and was expelled and, soon after, she walked out on me and in effect disappeared. As you may imagine, I was beside myself with worry and I even went to the police. They were sympathetic enough, but there was nothing they could do; they pointed out that by then she was sixteen and had a right to live on her own.'

'Do you know if she ever claimed the money she had been left?'

'I did try to find out, but the lawyers wouldn't divulge any information to me.'

'I assure you that we will do all we can to trace her and if we do find her, we'll try to persuade her to contact you. Any further questions you wish to ask, Mark?'

'Just one thing, Mrs Dickinson. Does a large glass paper-weight with flowers set in it mean anything to you? I only mention it as it was on the desk in your daughter Charlotte's office at the hospital.'

The woman's hand went to her mouth. 'Yes, James had one like that and it went missing from his study very soon after Charlotte went to stay with my brother. James made a great fuss about it, accusing the cleaning woman of having taken it, and she promptly gave notice. You don't think that Charlotte . . . '

'I was wondering if she might have taken it as a keepsake,' Sinclair said with a smile.

He saw the tears come into the woman's eyes. 'Yes, that must be it,' she said, 'and I'm so glad you told me; it shows that she didn't just have bad memories of him, don't you think?'

'Yes, I do.'

As the woman showed the two detectives out, she suddenly turned to face them.

'I know that you won't be able to guarantee it, but I have made a life here. I work for several charities and have made friends. Publicity would make things very difficult for me.'

'You have no need to be concerned from our point of view, but I'm afraid that the same can't necessarily be said about others. As I'm sure you know, the tabloids have very deep pockets, sources of information that are closed to us and not much in the way of conscience, so I fear there is no guarantee that they won't start ferreting around.'

'Yes, I do realize that and I'll just have to live with it.'

Sarah waited until they were back in the car. 'That's quite the most appalling and distressing story I've ever heard,' she said.

Sinclair nodded. 'I agree and may I say that you handled that interview quite beautifully. I really believe that our visit will have helped that poor woman to come to terms with what has happened and that's largely thanks to you. Why don't you give Tyrrell a ring this evening to let him know how we got on?'

Sarah nodded. 'We're due to meet those two solicitors tomorrow afternoon, so how about us fitting in a visit to Mrs Crawford's predecessor in the morning? The Crawford woman intrigues me — she's so anonymous, somehow, and not at all the sort of person I would have expected Helen Vaughan to engage.'

'Oh, I don't know. In the same way that very powerful men often seem to marry doormats who think that their husbands, however overbearing they may be, are wonderful, perhaps Helen liked to have someone who was just there, would do exactly what she was told and wouldn't challenge her in anyway. Anyway, I think it's a good idea of yours; the more information we're able to get on Helen Vaughan the better.'

8

Margaret Cassidy hadn't enjoyed herself so much for years. The visit of the police officers had given her the opportunity to get out the only really good pieces of china she possessed, the Royal Worcester cups, saucers and plates as well as the silver milk jug and teapot. It was not only that: when the local parson's wife called in early that morning, as she did most days, and heard that she was going to be entertaining guests, she immediately went back to the vicarage and brought back some homemade shortbread and a packet of McVities dark chocolate biscuits.

That wasn't the end of it. The tall, well-spoken inspector and his colleague, not some granite-faced woman, the like of whom she so disliked and who were almost routine in the TV detective series she was so fond of watching, was fresh-faced with a lovely smile and a well-rounded figure, quite unlike the anorexic models featuring in the magazines she took. And did she detect a hint of romance in the air? Surely the looks and little smiles they were giving one another were more than just friendly gestures.

'I couldn't believe it when I first heard what had happened to poor Helen Vaughan. She wasn't everyone's cup of tea, but one knew exactly where one was with her and I became very fond of her.'

'How did you come to be employed by her?' the young woman asked her.

'You could say that she inherited me. You see, I was housekeeper to her predecessor in the flat, Mr Bright, for several years after his wife died, but then he began to lose his memory and had to go into a nursing home. That's when Professor Vaughan bought the flat and she took me on as part of the furniture, so to speak.'

'I understand that the professor liked your successor to go into a guesthouse when she had visitors at weekends. Did you do the same?'

'No, I went to stay with my daughter in Esher. It used to happen quite often, but I thought it would be a mistake to go there permanently after I had to retire following my accident. Diana did offer, but she and her husband have two teenage children and it wouldn't have been fair on any of them.'

'How did the professor manage to find your successor, Mrs Crawford?'

The woman smiled. 'She didn't. I did the job for her!'

'You already knew her, then?'

'Yes, I remember very clearly where we first met. I was having a cup of coffee in the village. The place was very full and she asked if she could share my table. We got talking, arranged to see each other again and it went on from there. I won't say we were close friends, but we did meet about once a week.'

'What did you talk about?'

'I'm sorry to have to say that it was more of a question of what I talked about — always have been the most terrible chatterbox. She never said much, but perhaps that's why the professor was pleased with her — there was never any question of her gossiping. You see, the professor made it absolutely clear to me when I first worked for her that I wasn't to talk about her to anyone, particularly the other residents at the block. She was already getting well known and she told me that she wanted her flat to be a place where she would be able to escape from all the hassle and publicity. There were also tensions between her and some of the other flat-owners.'

'What was that about?'

'Oh, mainly her exclusive use of the roof terrace and sun room. Of course, she wouldn't budge and why should she? After all, she'd paid for it and if that awful man Cahill wanted it that badly, why hadn't he

166

bought it himself? The truth is that he couldn't afford to and he was just envious of the fact that a single woman clearly could. That man was and still is, no doubt, the archetypal MCP.' She gave Sinclair a warm smile. 'Not, of course, that I'm one of those equally tiresome women who put all men into that category.'

Sinclair smiled back. 'So, I imagine you never took Mrs Crawford or anyone else up to the flat.'

'Oh, no. The professor made it clear right from the start that I was never ever to do such a thing.'

'Did you know that Mrs Crawford was looking for a job as housekeeper?'

'No, it only came up after my accident when she made the offer to stand in for me until I recovered. What obviously clinched it with the professor was when I told her that Mrs Crawford was not only quiet and reliable, but that I knew that she had had secretarial experience. Then, when it became obvious that I was never going to be up to it again, the professor took her on permanently.'

'Do you still see her?'

'I did for a time, but gradually the intervals grew longer and then she stopped visiting altogether. I don't blame her and it's not as if

I'm lonely here. The very reverse — it's a lovely place.'

'What accident did you have?'

'I fell down and broke my arm when I was walking along the street near the shopping centre in Wimbledon. Enid thought that I had slipped on some wet leaves. She was holding my arm and my leg suddenly seemed to give way; I must have pulled her down because she fell on top of me, but fortunately she wasn't hurt herself. It was so lucky for me that Enid was there. She went with me to the hospital in the ambulance and while we were waiting for the X-ray, she could see how worried I was about having to let the professor down and she suggested that I ring her to tell her that she would be happy to stand in for me until I was fit again — she even had her mobile phone with her. It was all fixed up after the professor had inter-viewed her and had taken up her references. Enid was ever so good; she visited me every evening at St George's after they had operated on me.'

'Did Professor Vaughan visit you as well?'

'Oh, yes, she did, and brought me some really lovely flowers. I was so pleased and also that she liked Enid and what a bonus it was that she was able to do typing and other secretarial duties for the professor, which was quite beyond me. When it became obvious that I wasn't going to be up to getting back to work, I was delighted that Enid was able to take over completely.'

'Does Mrs Crawford have a family?'

'I don't know. All she told me was that she had lost her husband years ago, but as she obviously didn't want to talk about it, naturally I left it at that.'

'How did Professor Vaughan get on with the others in the block?'

'I don't know except for the fact that she and Mr Cahill were at daggers drawn, but then no one else got on with him either, and as to his poor wife! She was like a frightened mouse — I felt so sorry for her, but perhaps she likes being a doormat. Some people do, don't they? The only people in the block that I got to know were the Forbes and they are not the sort to gossip, at least not with the likes of me. Don't get me wrong, they are very nice people and were very kind to me. Mrs Forbes still visits me from time to time, but let me just say that there was just a hint of 'upstairs, downstairs' in their attitude towards me. It didn't bother me in the least; colonels and their wives are often like that, aren't they?'

Sinclair smiled. 'Very elegantly put, if I may

say so. Well, thank you so much for your help and the really lovely tea and shortbread. I haven't had anything as good in years, more's the pity.'

'Neither have I,' said Sarah. 'And if I had, I shudder to think what might have happened to this,' she added with a smile, patting her stomach.

The woman smiled. 'You've nothing to worry about, my dear. I think you look very nice, just as you are. I can hardly bear to look at these wafer-thin models these days — they're like pasty-faced stick insects.' She let out a throaty chuckle and then her facial expression changed abruptly. 'I do hope you find the brute who did that awful thing.'

★　★　★

The two detectives' first appointment, that with the solicitor in Southfields, took them less than ten minutes.

'Sometimes,' Henry Forrest, the senior partner of the firm, said, 'there can be difficulties when a solicitor is the sole executor, particularly if a will has been made many years earlier, and I don't normally recommend it. In this case, though, the professor, who was a very forceful person, made it quite clear that that was her wish, and she signed it only a few weeks ago. Her death, too, received so much publicity that there was no question of my having to make lengthy enquiries about potential beneficiaries, as is sometimes the case if, for example, the will was made a long time ago and those mentioned specifically in it have all died. In this particular case, it is also a help that you were able to find a copy in her effects. In fact, the will, as you no doubt have seen, is very simple and, apart from a donation to a research fund, everything has been left to one Emily Dickinson. I have her address and will be contacting her shortly.'

'I don't know whether you are aware that Professor Vaughan made an earlier will,' Sinclair said.

'I thought that was quite likely, but it was no business of mine to bring it up, not least because the professor was so definite in her requirements, and I neither enquired about it, nor did she make any allusion to it. I remember that she explained that her financial arrangements were not complex and that all the details were filed in her flat and that she had no plans to move in the foreseeable future. Should she do so, though, she undertook to let me know.'

'What intrigues me,' Sinclair said when

they were back in the car, 'is the identity of the woman who has been left out of that new will.'

'Me too. Why don't we go round to the address mentioned in the first will now? It's not far and we were such a short time with Forrest that we'll have plenty of time before our next appointment.'

'Good idea.'

The door of the small terraced house in New Malden was opened by a young woman with a baby on her hip.

'I'm afraid I can't help you,' she said in response to their query. 'You see, we bought this place from a couple who had just split up. They had left some weeks earlier and the house was completely empty. We never met them and all the paperwork was done between the solicitors.'

'Were you given a forwarding address?'

'Only the couple's solicitor and we never had to use it.' The young woman laughed. 'The post office must have been a great deal more efficient than they were when we moved; all we got was junk mail.'

'Do you remember their name, by any chance?'

'It's almost certainly in my address book. Would you mind taking Charlie while I have a look?'

'No funny remarks about being left holding the baby,' Sarah said with a grin, after the young woman had gone into a room off the hall. She cradled the little boy, who was staring at her intently with his dark brown eyes.

'The idea never crossed my mind.'

Sarah put out her tongue at him. 'Liar.'

The young woman came back a few minutes later. 'Yes, here we are. Jack Howe and Jean Redman. The only address is as I remembered; it's care of a firm of solicitors.'

'That's interesting,' said Sinclair, after they had thanked the young woman and were back in the car. 'It's the same firm we are just about to visit.'

On arrival at the second firm of solicitors, the two detectives were shown into an interview room and a few minutes later a tall, dark-haired woman, who looked to be in her middle thirties, came in.

'Inspector Prescott?'

'That's right, and this is my colleague, Inspector Sinclair.'

'I'm Angela King and I gather that you've come about Professor Vaughan's will.'

'Yes, that's right.'

'I was very shocked to hear about her violent death on the news — a tragic loss. Have you made any progress with your enquiries?'

'It's very early days as yet.'

It was hearing the woman speak that gave Sarah the first hint and now, looking at her more carefully, she suddenly realized where she had seen her before. The woman had been wearing a blonde wig and a variety of costumes and, often enough, no clothes at all and appeared in intimate detail in both the digital photos and the video in Helen Vaughan's flat.

'As you've no doubt seen,' the woman said, 'the will is quite simple and straightforward and she has left everything to Emily Dickinson, apart from some money to research projects and one bequest.'

'I understand that Emily Dickinson is Professor Vaughan's sister.'

'Yes, that's right. She went through a troubled time a few years ago and I was instructed to administer the allowance that Professor Vaughan made to her and, when she became financially independent, to keep an eye on her welfare.'

Sarah nodded. 'As it happens we're interested in that bequest.'

The woman looked up sharply. 'Why is that?'

'It's just that the will you have there is no longer valid.'

For a moment or two, Sarah thought that

the woman, who had gone ashen pale, was going to faint.

'I don't understand,' she said after a long pause.

'Professor Vaughan made a new will with another solicitor a few weeks ago. It is similar to the one you have there with the one exception that the previous bequest has been omitted and there is no mention of any direction of her sister's affairs. Do I take it from your reaction that you are also Jean Redman?'

'Redman was my married name and I used my maiden one for professional purposes after my divorce. Jean is my second forename.'

'In view of the fact that the bequest was to you, I must say I am surprised that you did not get one of your partners, or even a different firm of solicitors, to handle the will.'

'Helen Vaughan was a very close friend of mine right from our time at university together. I've already told you that there were considerable and very delicate problems to do with her sister, and she preferred me to handle it. She had every right to leave me some money and it was our joint decision that I should use my married name and not my professional one.'

'I see, and no doubt your close friendship

would also explain why we found so many photographs and videos of you in the professor's flat. Did you by any chance have a falling out with Helen Vaughan recently?'

'Of course not. How can you say such a thing?'

'Perhaps, then, you know of another explanation for her changing her will, in which case, we would be interested to hear about it.'

There was a very long pause. 'If you must know, we had a silly row — it wasn't as if it was anything serious. She accused me of having found someone else.'

'And had you?'

'Of course not. I loved Helen.'

'She must have had some reason for thinking it.'

'Just because I was in a bad mood and wouldn't go along with some plans she had for the two of us, she flew off the handle and it was just something she said on the spur of the moment. Helen was like that and we would have made it up again, I just know we would.'

'What sort of plans were they?'

There was a long pause and the woman dropped her eyes. 'She wanted me to take part with her in a group thing and that isn't my scene.'

'Do you have a solicitor of your own? I imagine that you don't employ one of your colleagues here, and we need to know what you were doing last Sunday evening between the hours of seven in the evening and midnight and it might be wise for you to be represented.'

There was a very long pause. 'That won't be necessary. I was alone in my flat.'

'Doing what?'

'I had supper over the *Antiques Roadshow*, read my library book, listened to some music, had a bath and went to bed at about eleven.'

'Where was the roadshow held? And perhaps you would tell me about some of the more striking pieces being shown?' Sarah made a note of her reply and then looked up. 'Would you also let me know your full name — the one you are using here — your address and home telephone number. We may well need to speak to you again and no doubt you would prefer us to do so there rather than here.'

The woman nodded, not meeting Sarah's gaze. 'About those photographs and videos . . . '

'Consideration of them will have to wait until we have completed our enquiries.'

★　★　★

The two detectives had supper at a pub in Wimbledon before setting out for Emily Dickinson's flat in Hammersmith and, by mutual consent, the case they were working on wasn't mentioned.

'Would you excuse me for a moment or two?' Sinclair said, after they had finished their coffee. 'I must make a couple of phone calls — nothing important, just personal matters.'

Nearly fifteen minutes went by before he reappeared. He was full of apologies. 'So sorry — it proved more complicated than I had anticipated. Shall we go?'

Emily Dickinson's flat was only a short walk from Hammersmith Broadway and was in the basement of a large terrace house. The outside looked as if it had been recently redecorated and the two detectives walked down the flight of stone steps into an area which was immaculate with some potted plants and two obviously new dustbins.

Sarah rang the bell and after a short pause, the external light was switched on and the door opened on a stout chain.

'Emily Dickinson?'

'Yes?'

'We are police officers and we'd like to speak to you about Helen Vaughan.'

Sarah showed her warrant card to the

young woman through the gap and, after a short pause, the chain was released.

'You'd better come in.'

Sarah had seen the school photograph of the girl when she would have been about fifteen and was quite unprepared for the young woman who faced her. Her body was better proportioned than that of her sister, which they knew only too well from the videos, and she was both taller and slimmer and was very pretty, her most striking features being her cornflower-blue eyes and blonde hair, which clearly had not been dyed or even touched up.

They were shown into a large and obviously newly decorated sitting room, which contained a sofa and two easy chairs. Against one wall, there was a desk and chair with a laptop, printer, telephone and fax on it, and on the opposite side a large bookcase. One shelf was occupied with large English, French and German dictionaries, other reference books including the *Oxford Companion to English Literature* and *Dictionary of Quotations*, while another had a collection of volumes on psychology and philosophy. There were abstract paintings on three of the walls and to the side of the curtained windows was a television with a DVD player on a shelf beneath it.

'Why not sit down over there,' the young woman said, 'and then you can tell me what this is all about.'

Sarah waited until Emily Dickinson was seated herself, thinking for one awful moment that the young woman might not know about Helen Vaughan's death and wondering how best to pose the question.

'You must have heard about the dreadful murder at the City Hospital?' To her great relief, the woman nodded almost imperceptibly. 'My name is Sarah Prescott, this is Mark Sinclair, and we're part of the team looking into the circumstances of Professor Vaughan's death.'

'How come you know about me? Was it through that solicitor?'

'Yes, but we were also able to trace your grandmother.'

'From the way you put it, I imagine that she told you that Helen was my mother — and what about my father?'

'That, too.'

'And will it become generally known?'

'Not if those particular circumstances had nothing to do with the murder.'

The young woman nodded. 'I've been wanting to talk to someone about this for ages and, what's more, someone who is neither a psychiatrist nor has an axe to grind.

Even though we've obviously only just met, I have an instinct about you. You see . . . '

★   ★   ★

Emily Dickinson's world fell apart the day, only a few weeks before her father died, when he was playing Scrabble with her. After they had finished adding up the score, he lay back against the pillows and beckoned to her, making a gesture towards the open door communicating with the adjacent room, where her mother was doing some ironing. It broke her heart to see him lying there looking so frail and he was so short of breath that every whispered word was an effort.

Emily had worshipped her father for as long as she could remember. He had been the one to help her when she was starting to read when she was four years old and with the rest of her school work later on, particularly with French and German. Like him, she had a talent for languages and he had made it such fun, a game in which they were able to communicate without her mother being able to understand what they were saying. She obviously resented it and Emily could never understand the reason why. He did jigsaws with her, taught her card games and, when she was older, draughts, chess and Scrabble.

It never occurred to her to question why she never went for walks with him on her own, or why she was never allowed to be alone with him in the house and that the door was always open whenever she was with him in his study. As he became frailer and frailer with his illness, some of these restrictions were relaxed, but the process had been so gradual that Emily hadn't noticed it.

'Come closer, dear, there is something I need to tell you before it's too late and I don't want her to hear,' he said, pointing to the door. 'Have you ever wondered why she's never let me be really alone with you?' Emily nodded. 'Well, you see, it was like this . . . '

It all came out. How Patricia had never been a proper wife to him, how headstrong and badly behaved Charlotte had been as a young child, getting up to mischief with the boy boarders and how he had punished her in the same way as them. How, as she grew up, their relationship had turned to one of love, and what that had led to.

The realization that Charlotte was her mother hit her with a force that was like a thunderbolt. It explained why Patricia was always hovering in the vicinity whenever she was with her father, why Charlotte had left home and disappeared and why her father and the woman she had thought was her mother were so distant and never showed any affection to one another. Emily remembered letting out one despairing cry and running out of the bedroom, and in the remaining few weeks of her father's life, she never spoke to him again.

She felt equally bitter towards both Charlotte and her grandmother. She started smoking cannabis with one of the other girls at Branscombe, who had a regular supplier, and from then on, things went from bad to worse. She was expelled from the school, ran away from her grandmother's new home and sank ever lower. She finished up in London in a squat, filthy dirty, covered in sores, with an STD, grossly underweight and addicted to heroin.

Emily had no idea how Charlotte found her — she didn't even recognize the woman with the black hair — but found she was and admitted to a private hospital, which specialized in the rehabilitation of drug addicts. She had not a single visitor during her stay and on several occasions came close to running away, but she did stick it out and the day before she was due to be discharged, the woman she came to know as Helen Vaughan, who had already made it crystal clear that that was what she wished to be called and that the name Charlotte Dickinson was never to be mentioned again, marched briskly into her room.

'I don't blame my mother for failing to protect me from my father,' she said. 'I don't believe she knew what was going on until I became pregnant and then, according to her lights, she did what she thought was best for all concerned. In that case, you might well ask why I decided to change my identity and not see her again. The answer is quite simple: I wanted to make a completely fresh start and take total control of my future. Not surprisingly, it didn't work entirely satisfactorily and my experiences with our father left me with certain needs that I have no intention of discussing with you.

'If you want my advice, you'll do as I did: stop feeling sorry for yourself and face the future in a way that suits you and no one else. I've made arrangements for my solicitor to collect you tomorrow and take you to your new flat, which has been fully equipped for you and which has twenty-five years of a lease to run. You will receive a generous monthly allowance from me until you get yourself organized and are able to deal in a sensible fashion with the money which your father left you. Angela King will also be able to help you with advice if there are any difficulties about that, or anything else. Now, don't be under any illusions about this; I will be keeping an eye on things and there is to be no drifting with the tide, no slipping back into the life you were leading, and if there is, that will be the end of it as far as I am concerned.

'You should understand that after today I don't propose to see you again and you're not to try to contact me unless there is some compelling reason. I have decided to give you the name I adopted and the address of the place where I work, partly because I suspect that it would not be too difficult for someone as bright as you obviously are to discover it yourself and also because I am impressed by the way you have stuck to it in this place. I trust you, but break that trust and that will be the finish as far as I am concerned. I shall also be very angry and it doesn't do to make me angry.

'Find a job and make the best of what, when all's said and done, is not such a bad deal. If you took a bit more care of your appearance, you'd be really pretty. You've got a good body and I have seen the results of the battery of psychological tests they've put you through here. You're right up there as far as intelligence is concerned and it's up to you to match that with application.

'As to your grandmother, she has managed to rise above the terrible things that have happened to her and is as happily settled as she could be under the circumstances. I don't blame her in any way for what happened — as I said before, she did her best as she saw it — and I must leave it to you to decide whether or not you wish to see her again. I have decided against that and expect you to respect my wish in that regard as well. Good luck.'

* * *

'And it has obviously worked out all right.'

'Yes, it has. I won't say that it was easy to start with and there were a number of occasions when I was so lonely that I nearly slipped back into taking drugs. However, there was always Helen's example to remember. I did my homework — perhaps she meant me to — and found out just how distinguished she had become in her field. What, after all, had I been through compared to her? I had been well cared for at home, I had had an excellent education up to the age of fifteen and even though I did lack a mother's love, which was as much my fault as that of my grandmother, who, heaven knows, tried as hard as she could to provide it. It was she who told me about the sexual abuse that Helen had had to put up with culminating in the pregnancy. In my stupid adolescent way, I thought my grandmother ought to have stopped it, but how could she when she didn't know about most of it, something I didn't believe at the time, but I do now. What am I going to do about her? I'll have to have a serious think about that. Why did I disintegrate when Helen so clearly didn't? I suppose the answer was that my personality wasn't as robust as hers.

'Anyway, it's no good dwelling on what Helen termed 'might have beens' and she was right. She gave me the opportunity to make something of my life and I wasn't going to waste it. Whereas Helen had a great talent for maths and science, as did her uncle, I had one for languages. I'd already had a good grounding with my father and at school, and after my rehabilitation I did further study at a language school, got a job with Lufthansa and I've even made a modest start with regard to my social life.'

'Did you know that Helen changed her will a few weeks ago? The two were almost the same in that in both she left the residue to you after a large bequest for research into DNA, but critically, she removed a legacy to Jean Redman — Angela King — in the second one. We found both wills in her flat.'

'No, I didn't know anything about a legacy,

let alone that it had been removed, but it doesn't surprise me. You see, I think it likely that I was responsible for that and there are other obvious possible implications, which I'll also clearly have to come to terms with. You would have thought that that solicitor woman would have given me a ring directly after Helen's death became public, wouldn't you? I never liked her. You see, she was the one who told me about Helen being beaten by her father. She was always trying to find out if the same thing had happened to me and when I got stroppy with her once, she made it plain that a good thrashing was what I needed, that it would clear the air and that she would be only too happy to oblige. I had experienced most things in my dark days and I knew her sort well. She wanted to try it on, all right — the whole thing, if you know what I mean.'

'You've lost me.'

The young woman smiled. 'I don't believe for one moment that I have, but I'll spell it out. In my bad times not only did I mix with addicts, psychopaths, sadists, masochists, psychotics, paedophiles, gays and rapists, but I have had to put up with an array of therapists, all masquerading under the prefix of psycho. Listeners, talkers, physical treaters, sympathizers and pull yourself togetherers have all had a go. I have become something of a dab hand at instant — I won't say diagnosis — categorization. That's why I knew what that woman was up to.'

'What did you do?'

'Told her that I wasn't interested and it was then that she gave me a detailed account of how she had met Helen at Cambridge and what had followed. I was so shaken and disgusted that I can remember what she said almost verbatim.

'She told me that she had already been a keen squash player when she arrived at her college in Cambridge to read law and was flattered when the captain of the women's team, Helen Vaughan, asked her if she would like a game and accepted with alacrity. On that occasion, the compact, quick-footed young woman was too quick for her and ran her round the court with her crisp shots. The contests became steadily closer the more they played, but Helen always had the edge.

'She said she had never forgotten the day it happened. She had run for a drop shot, just managed to execute a lob then, off balance, had just started to turn when she felt an agonizing pain high up on the back of her right thigh. She bent double, breathing hard, and as her hand moved back to rub the affected area, the leg of her shorts was raised and Helen's lips touched the bruised area.

' 'I'm so sorry,' Helen had said. 'I was watching the ball and didn't see that you were right in front of me.'

'In the changing room, which was empty apart from the two of them, when Helen came out of the shower, she dropped her towel and stood there without a stitch on. After staring at her for a moment or two, she walked across towards her opponent, removed the towel which the woman had secured above her breasts and let it fall to the floor. She felt inside her squash bag, took out a riding crop and held it out.

' 'You can get your revenge, if you like,' she said. 'I want you to.'

'Evidently, Helen turned round and bent over, resting her hands on the slatted bench. The first blow was hardly more than a tap.

' 'Harder, much harder,' she said.

'Without thinking and not really knowing what she was doing — at least, that's what she said — Angela drew back her arm and brought the crop down hard, right across the centre of her target.

'It went on from there.'

'How did you react to all that?' Sarah asked.

'Just told her that I wasn't interested,' Emily Dickinson replied. 'If she had left it at that, I would never have done anything further about it, but she didn't. She went on dropping hints, but then what had started as 'mwah mwah' kissing when she came in and left, very gradually went further until one day she tried to stick her tongue into my mouth and before I was able to extricate myself, she did other things with her hands, which I'll leave to your imagination. By that time, though, I had got a job and with that and the money coming from the investments that my father had left me, was financially independent. As I was in any case about to write to Helen to thank her and tell her that I no longer needed an allowance, I decided also to take the opportunity to inform her of exactly what Angela had done and said and that I was sure that she would understand that I never wished to see the woman again. I didn't have Helen's home address, so sent it to her at the City Hospital.'

'Did you get a reply?'

'No, but Angela didn't come again after that and my allowance was stopped.'

'When was that?'

'Roughly three months ago.'

'You will probably be relieved to hear that Angela King is no longer an executor or a beneficiary of the will — Helen made a new one recently with another solicitor. I don't think it right to give you the details apart from saying that you are the principal beneficiary — the new solicitor will be informing you of the details as they affect you very soon and I think you'll find that that woman, Angela King, won't trouble you again.'

Emily Dickinson nodded. 'From what you've said, it would probably be a good idea for me to get a solicitor and an accountant of my own and soon. You're no doubt wondering why I'm not more upset by Helen's death. Well, of course I am, but mainly on account of the great loss to science. You have to remember that I was only a baby when she left home and as a result, I have no memories of her at all, other than that of the brisk, no-nonsense woman who came to see me on that one occasion when I was in that hospital. The one person I do worry about is my grandmother and when the dust has settled over all this, I will have to decide what to do about her. Did you meet her yourself?'

'Yes, we both did and I have no doubt that seeing you again would be her dearest wish — but a decision about that will have to be yours and yours alone.'

'Have you any clues as to who killed Helen?'

'We've got a strong team working on it, but

it's far too early to expect any results. Very often to start with it's a question of eliminating possible suspects.'

The young woman's lips twitched. 'As I'm the main beneficiary of Helen's will, you will no doubt want to know what I was doing last Sunday night.'

Sarah smiled. 'That would be helpful.'

'I was at Heathrow from early evening until about 1 a.m. I was helping to sort out a major problem with mislaid baggage. An aircraft on a long-distance flight developed a fault, had to land in Kuwait and it was there that some of the luggage went missing. My job was to try to calm some of the distraught passengers.'

'Was it found?'

'Eventually.'

★ ★ ★

'I don't know about you, Mark, but I don't know how much more of this I can take without a break. I bet you Tyrrell has got something else for us up his sleeve — I suppose we'd better give him a ring.'

Sinclair grinned at her. 'I have a confession to make. You see, one of those calls I made at the pub was to him and, do you know what, he wants us to take a couple of days off to recharge our batteries, as he put it, after our testing week.'

'I don't believe it. And the other?'

'Ah yes, there were two, in fact. My brother-in-law lives near Marlow and has a cabin cruiser moored near there; from time to time he's rash enough to lend it to me and I was wondering if you would like to come on the river with me tomorrow and the day after?'

'Would I like? What a wonderful idea!'

'It's a good size and . . . '

'And what?'

'Would you also consider bringing your night things as well as a bathing costume? I won't have to return the boat until teatime on Sunday.'

'It gets better and better.'

'I'll pick you up at about eleven tomorrow morning, then. I have to go down to Rob's place first thing to get the keys and listen to the usual catalogue of dos and don'ts — they're off to a wedding in Devon and have to leave in good time. Oh, I almost forgot, the last call was to my mother and we've got a lunch date with her before we embark; she lives down that way and a visit from me is long overdue. Don't worry, there's no need to dress up and you'll like her, I know you will.'

9

Mrs Sinclair lived in a stone cottage on the edge of Cookham and they found her striding behind the motor mower on the substantial lawn. She had snow-white hair and from what Mark had said about her having been an army nurse in Germany after the war — where she had met his father, who was much older than her and a colonel in the army of occupation — she must have been in her late seventies. She most certainly didn't look it, Sarah thought.

'Come on, Ma,' Mark said, when he had done the introductions, 'let me finish that and you can show Sarah round.'

'This place is far too big for me, really,' the woman said when the two of them had gone into the hall, 'but I love it and so do the grandchildren. There are two of them, one four and the other two, and I have them one at a time. My daughter is a solicitor and my son-in-law in finance and they do have a full-time nanny, but the boy and girl are so different that I think it's good for both of them to have a day on their own here every week. James is a bit of a tearaway already and

Lucy rather quiet and timid, so their needs are very different. It's funny, isn't it, that being a grandmother is so much easier than being a mother? I'm sure that's not always true, but it certainly is in my case. I suppose that one of the reasons is that with me not being on top of them the whole time and their having more individual attention, they behave better here than they do at home.'

'Yes, I can understand that even though I never knew my grandparents. I was an only child and the man I thought was my father was rather crotchety; you see, he was really my stepfather and I only discovered that a few years ago, long after my mother died, which happened when I was fifteen. Anyway, after that I had to hold the fort, and if it hadn't been for my uncle taking me out from time to time and eventually arranging for him to go into a home soon after I joined the police force, I think I would have gone round the bend. He was very demanding and in that sense I had very little time to myself either. That's one of the reasons I like my work so much: having to think on my feet, being part of a team and meeting lots of different people.'

'Yes, I can see that. A bit like being a nurse and in the army, I suppose, which I was before I got married. I enjoyed that side of it, too.'

'The one big problem I've met is the class thing. You see, Roger Tyrrell, the head of our section, and Mark stick out, to say the least of it, and I suppose to some extent the same is true of me. The two men have had university educations, they speak in a different way from most of the others, they are well mannered, never swearing or shouting, they respect women and ethnic minorities, don't get drunk and what is the result? The others sneer at them, not to their faces, of course, but behind their backs, and it's not only the juniors, either. The toffs' army, the upper crust and the true blue brigade are some of the things we're called and as for Mark and me, we're known as M and S if they're being charitable and S and M if they're not. When I started I wasn't at all sure that I would be able to see it through. The initial training was all right, but after that was over and before I worked for Roger Tyrrell, I got stuck with the original MCP, I lost all confidence and I very nearly gave up as a result.'

'That's one of the reasons, too, why Mark moved to London,' Mrs Sinclair said. 'The Thames Valley people were exactly the same. You see, I know all about it myself; the army used to be very similar, only as far as I was concerned, it was the other way round. The regulars were an arrogant lot and not only did they resent the better educated National Service people, but even more, their fellow officers who had risen up through the ranks. You wouldn't believe the snobbery — the wives, too, were as bad or even worse than the men. I'm sure, too, that you must have been resented by the men.'

'That's certainly true, but the boot is now rapidly moving on to the other foot.'

The older woman smiled. 'You're only too right. I don't need to tell you that women's magazines used to be full of household tips, knitting patterns and decorous advice about how to keep your man happy. Now it's all empowerment, alternative medicine and bizarre sexual practices. Still, I have to confess I still read them. One has to keep up with the times, doesn't one? I can't bear old people who spend their whole time living in the past, wearing their rose-tinted spectacles. It wasn't all honeysuckle and strawberries and cream then, I can tell you.' Mrs Sinclair let out a tinkling laugh. 'I'm quite sure you didn't come here to make heavy conversation with an old has-been like me; Mark is always telling me that I talk too much. This is the drawing room, as I still like to call it.'

She opened the door to reveal a large, rectangular room, one side of which was taken up by French windows, which led on to a terrace with the lawn beyond it, and there was a large three-piece suite and two other easy chairs facing the fireplace. Against the wall to its left was a large grand piano.

'Mark likes to play on it when he's here, but his real love is the organ, which he studied when he was at Oxford. He doesn't get much opportunity for that these days, but he does occasionally play the instrument at our local church.'

As she went across to look at the photographs on the top of the piano, Sarah stopped short of it to tickle the sleek black cat behind its ear. The animal looked up at her with its yellow eyes and began to purr loudly.

'That's Henry. Mark had him from a kitten when he worked for Thames Valley Police. I was a bit doubtful about it as he lived alone in a flat, but it was on the ground floor and he fixed up a cat-flap and one of those food dispensers and it worked very well. Mark was a bit lonely at that time and I think Henry was a great comfort to him. He was very sorry to have to leave him with me when he went to London, but he had no alternative, really.'

'And that must be his wife?' Sarah said,

pointing to the picture of Mark standing, legs apart, near the edge of the sea, with a dark-haired young woman perched precariously on his shoulders.

The elderly woman picked it up. 'Yes, it was taken when Mark and Alex were on their honeymoon. Has he told you what happened?'

'Yes.'

'I'm so glad. One can never forget something like that, but there comes a time when one has to let go of the past and I was beginning to think he might never do so. It is a great relief to me to know that at long last he has achieved it.' Mrs Sinclair gave her a warm smile. 'Let's see how the baked spuds are getting on, shall we?'

★   ★   ★

'Have a good time,' Mrs Sinclair said, as she opened the front door for them. 'Don't go and get yourself burnt, will you, Sarah? It's so easy to do so on a day like this, especially on the river. I've put some sun cream in with the tea I've got for you in this.' She lifted up the large wicker basket, covered by a tea towel. 'Don't worry about the basket, or the containers in it; you can always return them later.'

'Thank you so much,' Sarah said, putting her arms round the woman's shoulders and giving her a kiss. 'You shouldn't have bothered, particularly after that lovely lunch.'

'You made a real hit with Ma, you know, Sarah,' Sinclair said, as they joined the main road.

'Did I?'

'Yes, you certainly did. She can't bear what she calls the droopy, anorexic brigade, who can't get up in the morning and have a total obsession with clothes and shopping and whose idea of a good lunch is a carrot with a garnish of tired lettuce.'

Sarah let out a giggle. 'Well, anorexic is certainly not something that can be said about me.' She raised her eyebrows as she patted her stomach. 'Seriously, though, I thought she was lovely, really great.'

'Yes, it can't have been easy for her. You see, my father was more than twenty years older than her, but they had a great marriage and she always knew that she was likely to have a long widowhood. Marrying again was never an option for her; she wanted to be there for the three of us and any grandchildren and always has been. I just knew you'd like her.'

*   *   *

When Sinclair had taken off the cover, Sarah saw that the boat was a great deal larger than she had expected, with two seats set up high on a platform behind the wheel, and the well, astern of that, was surrounded on three sides by a bench with a padded surface. The cabin was also substantial with two bunks on either side of a stowable table and in the bow was a shower and lavatory, with a single cabin to its side.

'This is pretty well designed,' Sinclair said. 'As you can no doubt imagine, the arrangement as it is set up now is more than a bit of a passion killer, but don't worry, with a bit of judicious adjustment, a more than adequate double bed can be fashioned out of it.'

Sarah raised her eyebrows. 'Thank goodness for that. Do your sister and brother-in-law ever take it out into the open sea?'

'Yes, they used to, but not now with two young children. It's fitted with a satellite navigation system and they used to go across to the Normandy and Brittany coast most summers. I'm sure they'll do so again before long; Ma has already volunteered to have both children to stay, but Lucy's still a bit too young for that.'

After he had checked the fuel gauge and re-familiarized himself with the controls, Sinclair started the engine and within a few minutes they were proceeding slowly upstream.

'Why not hop up on to the deck, have a lie in the sun for a bit and I'll give you a shout when we're approaching the first lock? It's quite interesting if you've not been in one before.'

It was. Sarah watched with interest and admiration at Mark's skill as he edged the large boat right up to the one in front. Then, when the gates closed behind them, they progressed upwards until they were able to continue onwards. Once they were through, she lay back against the cushion, pulled her sunhat over her eyes, experiencing feelings of happiness and relaxation, the like of which she had never felt before.

'Sarah!' She woke with a start to see Mark beckoning to her. 'You'd better come inside now, you're looking distinctly pink.'

She stayed where she was for a moment, stretching and yawning, then, looking round, saw that Mark had moored the boat half under a willow tree and crawled back along the deck.

'Why not go into the cabin and I'll put some cream on your back and shoulders?'

She could hardly see at first and then when her eyes became adapted to the gloom, saw that he had laid a large towel on the table, with a cushion on top of it.

'Stand here and stretch yourself out. Put your head on this, then grip the other side.'

He undid the straps of her bikini top and began to massage the cream into her shoulders and back with a gentle circular motion.

'My goodness, you are hot,' he said, 'dangerously hot, and there's only one cure for that.'

She knew exactly what he meant as he slipped her bikini bottom down and freed it from her legs, anticipating what was to come, then she let out a high-pitched shriek of surprise at the extraordinary feeling that shot right through her, followed by a more familiar one that sent her into a state in which she hardly knew what she was doing. Sarah let herself go completely, only vaguely aware that she had cried out and that there were strange noises coming from behind her.

Sarah came back to full awareness, to find herself lying on the table, with a thin blanket on top of her.

'I'm just going to pop into the shower. Why not stay there until I'm through and then you can do the same.'

Sarah only came to properly when Mark reappeared, rubbing himself briskly in a thick towel.

'I should warn you that the water's bloody

cold in there to start with, but after that, it's bliss.'

He was right. When she came out of it, she was tingling all over and went outside to see Mark sitting under the canopy at the stern of the boat, which he had opened up and laid out the small table beneath it. There were raspberries in glass bowls, a jar of clotted cream, buttered scones and strawberry jam and a bottle of Liebfraumilch in an ice bucket.

Sarah picked one of the ice cubes out of the bucket between her thumb and forefinger and held it up in front of her.

'So that is what it was, was it, you terrible man?'

'Guilty,' Sinclair said, holding up his hand. 'I read somewhere that it was the ultimate sensation and I couldn't resist the opportunity.'

'I see. Has anyone ever tried it on you?'

'Not yet.'

Sarah raised her eyebrows. 'A pleasure in store, perhaps?' She stared at him with mock severity. 'Well, when are you going to crack that bottle?'

'Am I forgiven, then?'

'Forgiven? It was the most fantastic feeling I've ever experienced, not, though, I hasten to add, to be repeated other than on very special occasions, such as this.'

When he had poured out the wine, Sarah raised her glass.

'To us and your mum. If this is a little tea, I can't help wondering what a big one is like.'

'Something to experience and like the ice cube, not very often.'

After proceeding further upstream for another half hour or so, Sinclair tied the boat up at a jetty close to a riverside pub and after a long walk along the towpath, they had a leisurely supper outside. For the first time since she had started to work on it, Sarah managed to put the case right out of her mind and the day ended with them making warm and gentle love on the big double bed in the cabin.

The following morning might have been an anticlimax, but it wasn't. There was orange juice, scrambled egg and bacon, toast, butter and marmalade and coffee at the pub and afterwards, Sarah was given a lesson in driving the boat.

'The biggest challenge,' Mark said, 'is learning control of the motor. To start with, although it's so obvious when you think about it, you have to remember that the only ways to reduce speed are to throttle back and to throw the engine into reverse. Looking ahead and anticipating possible problems are even more important than driving a car. You may think that there is so much more time and although that's true, the boat takes a long time to react. At least you've got a wheel rather than a tiller; lots of people find the latter a real problem to start with. Pushing it away from you in order to go left, or perhaps I should say to port, is an easy enough concept to understand, but one has to learn how to do it without thinking. It's a bit like reversing a car, which most people find difficult to start with. Right, you know where the important controls are, you know the rules when passing any other boat and the speed limits, so now she's all yours.'

The great thing, Sarah was to think later, was that Mark didn't nag or overdo the instructions and cautions, even to the extent of disappearing into the cabin for a few minutes on one occasion. As a result she rapidly developed a degree of confidence. The experience also gave her an entirely different perspective on the difficulties of manoeuvring the boat into and out of the locks and even more so when he returned it to its mooring.

'Thank you so much for letting me have a go,' she said, giving him a kiss after he had given the boat a final once-over and the tarpaulin was in place. 'I'm not pretending that I had to do very much, but it was a great thrill none the less.'

'You have a real feel for it, one can always tell. It's like your driving; I'm not the greatest passenger normally, but with you I can even fall asleep sometimes, which is a first for me in that situation. That's not the only thing you're good at, either.'

Sarah felt herself blushing, then laughed. 'I think 'we' would be more appropriate, don't you?'

★ ★ ★

In Tyrrell's office at the Yard the following morning, after he had given his report, Sinclair looked across at Sarah, half listening to what she was saying, and the feeling that he had thought he would never experience again went right through him. Something also made him glance towards his superior and immediately he was quite sure that the man knew exactly what he and Sarah had been doing at the weekend. It wasn't a look of disapproval, or censure, and certainly not prurience, just quiet amusement, almost as if a prediction had proved to be correct. Of course the man had noticed, how could he have failed to do so? Sarah had a glow about her, which was much more than just the reaction to all the sun, fresh air and the excitement of the river trip. She radiated contentment and the sheer joy of being alive and in love. Sinclair was profoundly embarrassed by what Tyrrell was obviously thinking, despite knowing that he had no real cause to be, at the same time realizing that a lot of his reticence had been inherited from his father, who had always shied away from outward displays of emotion. His mother, though, had hinted often enough that there were fires burning beneath that formal and at times even forbidding exterior.

'Right,' Tyrrell said crisply, when Sarah had finished, his expression now serious and alert. 'Where do we stand? It seems as if the unpleasant Cahill is in the clear, as is Emily Dickinson, if her alibi stands up. Have you had the opportunity to check it yet, Sarah?'

'Yes. I got on to the airline first thing this morning and they confirmed everything she'd said.'

'Good work. Anything to add, Mark?'

'I'm intrigued by Helen Vaughan's housekeeper, Mrs Crawford. We know that she only took an overnight bag with her when she went off to the bed and breakfast place in Putney and yet there was almost nothing left behind in her bedroom, just a few clothes and virtually no personal possessions. She has, after all, been there for a good eighteen months and according to Mrs Forbes had no visitors and hardly went out other than to the shops. And then there is the question of her predecessor's accident, or was it an accident? The Crawford woman was there at the time so was it an elaborate plot to insinuate herself into Helen Vaughan's life?'

'Hmm. That sounds a bit far-fetched to me and Helen Vaughan did indeed ring her briefly very soon after seven on the evening she was killed. We were able to find that out through the telephone company.'

'I see, but I still think it's worth checking her out through her references. The photocopies of them are in the file.'

'Have you got them there?'

Sinclair passed them across the desk and after he had scrutinized them, Tyrrell looked up.

'Hmm, the Reverend Henry Glanville and Mrs Margot Forrest from Cladenham in Sussex. Never heard of the place. How about you, Mark?'

'I hadn't, either, but I looked it up on the internet earlier this morning. Hassocks is the nearest town and evidently its main claim to fame is an eighteenth-century church that's mentioned in one of Pevsner's books.'

'I see. Well, both references say much the

same sort of thing: knew her well, reliable, helpful and did sterling work for the church and local charities. What do you think, Sarah?'

'It is a bit of a long shot, but like Mark, I thought the Crawford woman was more than a bit strange and I'm sure it would be worthwhile paying those referees a visit to get some background on her. After all, we haven't much else to go on.'

'Very well, then,' Tyrrell said, 'why don't the two of you handle that today? The other thing that concerns me still is McKenzie. From what you discovered from Spencer and the dean, it seems that his attitude to Helen Vaughan changed completely after that girl's suicide and perhaps you'd see what you can find out about her; I was thinking of the inquest as a start.

'That leaves us with that solicitor, Angela King, otherwise known as Jean Redman. From what you told me on the phone, Mark, something very obviously went wrong with her relationship with Helen Vaughan recently, what with the arrival of a new playmate and the alteration of the will. Emily Dickinson clearly couldn't stand her, particularly when she tried to recruit her into her particular perversion, and the woman has no real alibi for the evening in question — she could easily have recorded that particular *Antiques Roadshow* and watched it the following day. What do the two of you think about her?'

'She's certainly a powerfully built woman and would have had the strength to have delivered the blow that killed Helen,' Sinclair said, 'but I'm pretty certain she didn't know about the will having been changed. However, perhaps Helen confronted her with what she had tried on with Emily Dickinson and told her that their relationship was over. If that's the case, she had an obvious motive, but would she have done it in such a calculated way? I don't think so. In the first place, how would she have known that Helen was going to be at the hospital on that particular evening and how would she have got into the pathology department without Helen letting her in? Surely, too, she would have cooked up at the very least a more convincing alibi for the time in question.'

Tyrrell nodded. 'What you say makes good sense. Right, see what you can do in Cladenham and let's meet here again on Thursday morning. I've got this wretched seminar on 'Racism in the Met' for the next couple of days. All right?'

★ ★ ★

'Yes, of course I remember Enid Crawford.'

The vicar of Cladenham, the village in West Sussex, was a short, portly and benign-looking man, who was wearing a grey suit and a dog collar. Although, Sinclair thought, he must have been all of sixty, his face was unlined and he beamed at them over the top of his half-moon spectacles. 'So you're trying to get hold of her, is that right?'

'Yes. We are trying to trace her over a will,' Sinclair said, 'and the only line we have to pursue is that of the two people who wrote references for her for a job in London roughly eighteen months ago, namely you and a Mrs Forrest.'

'Is Enid Crawford a beneficiary of this will?' He gave a loud chuckle, his very blue eyes twinkling as he looked at the detective. 'But you won't tell me the details, will you? You lot are as tight with information as Father O'Connell from the next village. He's always trying to make me introduce confession here. Some hopes; I've never been a devotee of that kind of soul-searching, let alone to a fellow who thinks that downing a glass of whisky is a mortal sin. Irish priests on the television and in films are almost always depicted as round, jolly men, worldly-wise and tolerant of the weaknesses of others and enjoying a snort or two, but not him, oh dear me no. You should see his expression when good living is even hinted at! Steeped in vinegar would be the best description.' He laughed when he saw the look on Sarah's face. 'You mustn't take what I say too seriously, you know, my dear. Enough of this idle chatter — I'll have to see what I wrote in that reference, if, that is, my filing system is up to it.'

'That's all right,' Sinclair said. 'I have a photocopy of your letter here.'

He took it from the detective, studied it for a moment and then looked up, raising his eyebrows.

'I see you've blacked out the name of the person to whom I sent it. 'Curiouser and curiouser, said the white rabbit.' ' He gave them a broad smile. 'I mustn't tease you and I'm quite sure it was done for a very good reason. The will of someone very well known, perhaps? Only joking and I doubt very much if I'll be able to find my copy — I'm not even sure that I kept it. You'd better watch out for Margot Forrest, though. Unlike me, she's as sharp as a needle and so organized that I'm quite sure that she keeps all her supermarket receipts in chronological order for at least ten years.

'Enough of this, I always did use a dozen words where a couple would do; you should ask all those who fall asleep in my sermons. Tell me what you want to know.'

'Just anything you are able to remember about her, in particular any personal details, such as her family and where she came from.'

'I'll do my best, but Margot will be a better bet — she likes a good gossip, does Margot. Well, after all that, you might be surprised to hear that I remember her quite well. You see, she turned out to be quite a dab hand with the flower arranging and was also an expert at tapestry and other forms of needlework, both of which came in very handy at the church. She did the flowers for all the weddings and other special occasions and organized a group of the local women to cooperate in the making of a large quilt, which was eventually sold as part of the fund-raising for the reconditioning of the organ.'

'Did you know her personally?'

'No more than with our contacts over church matters. She was very conscientious, but I wouldn't call her exactly a bundle of fun, or even the merest ray of sunshine. A very serious person, she was, never seeming to get the point of the little jokes I am guilty of inflicting on people from time to time.'

'Do you know where she came from?'

'No and I never asked, but I wouldn't be surprised if it wasn't somewhere rather like this place. You see, in her particular way, she fitted in rather well here. I take it you haven't met her?'

Sinclair inclined his head slightly, which, as he had hoped, the man obviously took as a 'no'.

'If you had, I think you'd understand. In my hearing, she never once offered anything about her personal life. Where she came from, what she used to do before she arrived here and details of her family were a completely closed book.'

'Well, thank you for your help.'

The man smiled. 'You know and I know that I haven't been the slightest help, but don't worry, I appreciate the niceties — they keep people happy. But a word of warning: don't try it on with Margot, she's not one for that sort of thing.'

Although they had learned nothing of any importance, Sarah had been quite taken by the vicar, although she would probably have liked him a good deal less had she known that directly they had gone, he went straight to his laptop, entered the file marked 'References' and found that his letter about Enid Crawford had been addressed to one Professor Helen Vaughan. Not only that, he was not one of those otherworldly parsons who didn't own a television set and only read the leaders and obituaries in *The Times*: he knew perfectly well who Helen Vaughan was and what had happened to her.

Margot Forrest was a brisk, formidable-looking woman, who appeared to be in her late fifties. She had a tightly permed head of hair and with her tweed skirt and stout brown shoes, looked as if she was about to stride across the downs with the black labrador, which was sitting, thumping the parquet floor in the hall with its tail, more in the hope than the expectation that he was going to be taken for a walk.

'I see,' she said, when they were sitting in the drawing room and Sarah had explained that they needed to contact Enid Crawford about a will and that she'd gone away without, as far as they'd been able to ascertain, telling anyone why or where.

'Is she a beneficiary of this will?'

'I'm afraid that I'm not able to give you any details about that.'

'Of course, I shouldn't have asked.'

'Did you know her well?'

'As well as anyone here, I suppose, and I was only too happy to recommend Enid Crawford and I was very concerned for her when I heard the dreadful news about Professor Vaughan. I didn't immediately remember why the name was familiar and then it came to me and I was able to confirm that she was the person who wrote to me for the reference.'

'You say very concerned. May I ask in what way that was?'

'Well, she did tell me that the reason she came here — it must have been about four years ago — was because she wanted to escape from the town where she had lived all her married life.'

'Did she say why?'

'She wasn't one to talk about herself, but she did hint at domestic tragedies. She refused to elaborate, but she did say that she had had a bereavement of someone close to her and she couldn't stand the way people treated her.'

'In what way?'

'Evidently they seemed embarrassed by her, not treating her as a normal person and passing by on the other side of the road whenever they saw her approaching. She didn't have an exactly warm personality and although that's no excuse for their behaviour, I can understand it. She could be very abrupt, could Enid Crawford. Anyway, having suffered that sort of trauma, the violent death of her employer would, I imagine, have hit her very hard.'

'Did she fit in well here?'

'She did and she didn't. She was a tremendous help to me in my charitable work here, particularly that associated with the local church. She had secretarial skills, including word processing, and that was an enormous bonus in the preparation of the village magazine, which I started a few years back. However, she wasn't good at making friends.'

'Did she use your machine, or did she have one of her own?'

'She used mine.'

'Does it include an internet connection?'

'Yes, she sometimes looked up things for me — I write a column on country matters for one of the national women's magazines as well as for the local one here.'

'Where did she live here?'

'She had a bed-sitting room at one of the local farms and Mrs Russell also provided some simple cooking facilities for her as well as breakfast. Mrs Russell is a great talker, but I can't imagine that she got anything out of Enid. In fact, the arrangement suited them both, as it didn't interfere with the bed and breakfast set-up she also has there.'

'In view of what happened to her before, how do you suppose she would have coped with yet another tragic event?'

'I just don't know, but it's tempting to

think that she might have reacted in the same way as she did before by taking off without telling anyone about it.'

'You mean that when she left her previous home, she didn't tell anyone where she was going.'

'She didn't say that to me directly, but you know what country villages are like and Fred Dixon, the local postman, told me once when she had been here about a year that she hadn't received a single personal letter, only junk mail and notifications of local events.'

'In that case, how do you suppose she managed her financial affairs?'

'I've no idea and if you'd met her, you'd know it wasn't a question I could possibly have asked her. I suppose she must have had an accommodation address somewhere and now I come to think of it, she might have used my Internet connection here. I did tell her she was welcome to do so for her own purposes if she so wished.'

'Did you correspond with her or even ring her up after she left here?'

'Only when she wrote to ask if I would act as a referee for her and then some time later to thank me and to say she had got the job.'

'Was she happy here?'

'Happy is not a word I would use with regard to Enid Crawford, but I do believe she was reasonably content. I say that because I always found her ever helpful and polite, although very reserved. I respected that and I think that's one of the reasons why we got on well.'

'Why do you suppose, then, that she left here and went to London?'

'I'm not absolutely certain, but I think she needed the money; she did let slip once that her husband had left her very little after the debts had been paid off.'

'But why London?'

'Partly the anonymity, I suppose, and jobs for women of that age just don't exist around here unless it's cleaning. She told me she had a friend up there and was going to stay with her while she looked round. It must have been quite a struggle, because, as I recall, it must have been a good two months before she wrote to ask me if I would act as a referee for her.'

'And you haven't heard from her recently?'

'As I said, the only time I heard from her was the thank you letter I mentioned just now, it must have been at least a year ago, I'd say.'

'Do you put photographs in your local magazine here?'

'That's Henry Cartwright's province. He's a widower, a retired general practitioner, and it's his main hobby. He does still and video and I must say the results are brilliant. Lots of people are competent photographers, but he also has a real gift for editing.'

'Do you think he has a picture of Enid Crawford? It would be a great help to us.'

'I think it unlikely, as for some reason she had a strong dislike of being photographed. Why don't you ask him? He lives just up the road and he'll welcome any conversation about his pet obsession, believe you me. I'll give him a ring if you like.'

The woman was as good as her word and, after thanking her for her help, the two detectives walked the hundred yards or so to the thatched cottage set back a little from the road.

Henry Cartwright was a tall, very thin man, who looked to Sarah to be in his late seventies. He may have been rather bent and with arthritic fingers, but there was both intelligence and a twinkle in the light grey eyes, which peered at her over the top of his half-moon spectacles.

'Two detectives, no less, and from Scotland Yard,' he said, when Sinclair had made the introductions. 'This is an unexpected treat. Come in. I'm just brewing some coffee, not some of the instant muck, mind you, the real thing, Colombian, and with a real bite to it.

Nothing like it for geeing up tired neurons, but I'm quite sure that yours won't have reached that stage yet. Sit yourself down in here and I'll be with you in just a shake of a dog's tail.' He laughed as he saw Sarah's expression. 'Don't worry about my 1930s slang: much more picturesque and elegant than the lavatorial stuff that's the vogue these days.'

When the man reappeared a few minutes later with a tray, on which were three bone china cups and matching coffee pot, with some cream in a silver jug and a plate of ginger biscuits, Sinclair, who had been tickling the large tabby cat, which was lying on one of the chairs, stood up straight.

'You like cats?'

'Yes, I do, very much.'

'So do I. Do you know what Montaigne said about his cat?'

'*"Quand je joue à ma chatte, qui sait si elle passe son temps de moi, plus que je ne fais d'elle."*'

There was a pause while the man looked at Sinclair in amazement, then he let out a loud guffaw.

'What a pity that Rachel isn't here to have heard me getting my come-uppance. She was always taking me to task for showing off. Are you also a linguist and *au courant* with

French philosophers, too, my dear?'

'I'm afraid not. You see, I didn't read modern languages at Oxford like my colleague.'

'He did that, did he? In that case, I'll have to watch my Ps and Qs, won't I? It means: 'When I play with my cat, who knows whether she is getting more fun out of it than me.' Very true, don't you think? Bessie there is a great consolation to me.'

'As my cat was to me,' Sinclair said. 'I was very sad to leave him with my mother when I moved to London, but at least he's in good hands.'

The man poured out the coffee, sat down opposite them on the other side of the occasional table and looked up alertly.

'So you want a picture of the mysterious Enid Crawford?'

'Yes. As I explained to Mrs Forrest, we are trying to trace her on account of a will. We know that she moved to London from here and she is no longer at the one address we had for her there.'

'I see. Curiouser and curiouser. Well, I do have a photograph of her all right and the getting of it is of some interest. As Margot probably told you, I spice up her admirable gazette by taking pictures and putting them into the text using my equipment here. I wander round at local functions snapping away and anything amusing or of interest gets an airing. Everyone knows what I'm up to and Enid Crawford was the first person I've come across who's objected. At one of the charity bring and buys, soon after she came here, I had just packed the digital camera away, having got the shots I wanted, when I saw the Crawford woman bending over inspecting an exotic plant in one of the stalls. She had the most marvellously snooty expression on her face and I took a couple of shots of her with my old Leica, which was on a strap round my neck.

'She must have heard the click, because she turned on me like an avenging Fury.' He smiled at Sarah. 'Do you know about the Furies, my dear?'

'No, I don't.'

'They come from Greek mythology and were snake-haired goddesses, who pursued unpunished criminals. No doubt you do the same, my dear, but I'm quite sure in a more gentle fashion and without that unbecoming hairstyle. I digress. Anyway, she hissed at me — she really did, you know — saying that no one took her photograph without asking first and demanded that I let her have the negative at once. So I gave her the whole roll — in fact, it only had those two exposures on it

— and she promptly pulled it out of its cassette and threw it into the nearest litter bin. What she clearly didn't know, though, was about the magical properties of digital cameras and the fact that I had another picture of her, which I can show you on the screen of my laptop.'

'Why do you think she behaved like that?'

'I don't know exactly, but I made it my business to do some research on her with some of the locals. What I learned was that she kept herself to herself. No one, not even Margot, who could prise secrets out of a clam, knew where she came from, or what she was about, which is one of the expressions you young people like to use, I believe.'

'What did you make of her yourself?'

'As an ex-GP, and I'm quite sure that Margot would have told you about that, I did have some experience of oddballs and my guess is that she is an obsessional neurotic, someone with a mountain of complexes. Did you know that some of them will wash their hands almost continually? When they've finished scrubbing away, they may inadvertently touch something before using the freshly laundered towel and back they go to the same ritual. I have seen them with hands that are almost raw.

'Anyway, on the occasion of the photograph to which she took such exception, the Crawford woman may have thought that I had captured something unbecoming in her posture or clothing as she bent over. Who knows, perhaps she has a horror of exhibiting her VPL?' He let out a chuckle as he saw Sarah's raised eyebrows. 'I'm not quite so out of touch with reality as you might think, my dear.'

'I'm quite sure you're not.'

Sarah watched as he brought up the series of coloured images on the screen.

'Yes, here we are. There she is, talking to the vicar. It was after the service to commemorate the life of one of the local teenagers, who was killed in a car crash. You've never heard such hyprocrisy; he was painted as some sort of golden boy with the world at his feet, whereas he was a tearaway who was quite out of control. Drink, a variety of drugs, driving without a licence or insurance, sex with underage girls, you name it, he did it. And just because he was the son of a local landowner, who is also a keen supporter of the church, Henry Glanville went ahead with it — he would, though, he's a pusillanimous nonentity, if you ask me.' Sarah was just thinking that it was another word she would have to look up, when he saw

227

her expression of incomprehension. 'Sorry, m'dear, I know I shouldn't use words like that, but I very much regret how limited people's vocabulary has become. It means characterized by a lack of courage or determination; I'm quite taken by it, it has such a fine ring to it.'

'It certainly does; I must bring it out sometime and shake my superiors with it.'

The man let out another guffaw. 'Good for you.'

The picture had been taken from the side and there was a clear three-quarter view of the woman's face. Her black hat, despite being pushed back slightly towards the back of her head, obscured her face to some extent, but none the less the woman was instantly recognizable.

'I expect you'd like me to run off a couple of shots.'

'Would you? It's just the sort of thing we're after.'

'I could give you an enlargement of her face, too, if you like.'

When he showed them to the gate a few minutes later, they thanked him warmly.

'The thanks should be entirely mine,' he said. 'It's been a real pleasure meeting you both.'

'What a splendid old boy,' Sarah said as

they walked to her car, having no doubt that he really did mean what he'd said. Old he may have been, but there was still a sparkle about him and she was quite sure that in his day he would not have been in the least short of admirers. 'How on earth did you manage to come up with that quotation? It was brilliant.'

'Pure luck. My mother knew how much I was missing my cat and sent me a little book full of pictures and quotations. The one that old boy mentioned happened to be one that took my fancy and it stuck in my memory. I also did some work on French philosophers as part of my course at university and Montaigne struck a chord.'

'Well,' Sarah said, raising her eyebrows, 'all that sort of stuff is well outside my league. I suppose we'd better tackle Enid Crawford next.'

'Wouldn't it be wise to wait until after we've talked it over with Tyrrell on Thursday? We could fill in the time by seeing if we can find out a bit more about the girl who committed suicide. That pathologist fellow, Spencer, made it fairly clear that that dreadful business was responsible for raising the level of dislike between McKenzie and Helen Vaughan. We've got the address of her mother — as I recall it was somewhere in

Luton. We could go tomorrow.'

'Good idea and why don't I ring Miss Tombs when we get back and see if she'd fax me a report of the inquest and post mortem? Do you remember that that fellow Tranter told us that Tredgold had done the autopsy on the girl?'

'So he did. I'll see if I can get hold of a photograph of the girl from the medical school. If her mother has moved, it might come in useful.'

10

'Any luck with the photograph of Rebecca Turner?' Sarah asked when she met Sinclair back at her flat that evening.

'Yes. All the new intake of students at the City Hospital have their photographs taken and they are stored on CDs.'

He handed the print across and Sarah looked at it carefully.

'Hmm. She must have been about eighteen or thereabouts when this was taken and she looks like a refugee from the 1950s and very young for her age. Whatever must the others have thought about that hairstyle?'

'How about the inquest?'

'I've got the transcript here. Evidently the girl's mother said that her daughter had just finished her house job at one of the hospitals quite near their home and was staying with her while waiting for her interview at the City Hospital for her next post. Pathology was what she really wanted to do and she was very excited at having been shortlisted and granted an interview. She had left the house that morning full of optimism about the future. She had telephoned directly after she had been turned down for the post. She was obviously distraught and almost incoherent and kept on apologizing for letting her mother down, that she wasn't worthy of her and that there was no way that she would be able to repay her for all the sacrifices she had made on her behalf.

'Mrs Turner tried to keep her talking, but the young woman rang off. Desperately worried about what her daughter might have gone on to do, she dialled 999, told them what had happened and heard the dreadful news less than an hour later. Rebecca had been found in one of the lavatories in the students' hostel at the City Hospital, where she had lived when a student. One of the residents there had seen blood trickling under the door and raised the alarm. The autopsy revealed that apart from the injuries to her wrists, the young woman had otherwise been healthy. After the dean had stated that Rebecca had shown no signs of depression when she was a student and that he was satisfied that the interview for the pathology post had been conducted fairly and sympathetically, the coroner brought in the verdict that Rebecca Turner had taken her own life whilst the balance of her mind had been disturbed by her failure to get the post on which she had set her heart. He then went on to express his sympathies to the bereaved mother.'

★   ★   ★

The street on the outskirts of Luton had rows of terraced houses on both sides which had clearly all been built at the same time, the only signs of individuality being different coloured front doors and a variety of hideous covered-in porches. All of them had tiny front gardens bisected by a short path, some of which were well tended, others a mass of tangled weed, and in a few the whole had been obliterated and covered by asphalt or concrete, to make a parking area just large enough to accommodate a small car.

The young woman who answered the bell of the address they had been given was carrying a small baby and shook her head when Sarah showed her the photograph of Rebecca Turner and explained that they were trying to trace her.

'She was here about four years ago, you said? We've only had the house since my husband got a job at the airport a couple of years ago and we never met the previous owner. Steve dealt with the sale with the estate agent and a solicitor.'

The powerful young man wearing a T-shirt

and jeans who appeared in answer to her call wasn't able to help either.

'No, the couple who were here before us had just split up. We never met either of them and I've no idea where they are now.'

'What about your neighbours? Have any of them been here for long?'

'Not the people on either side of us, but you might try the bloke across the road. He spends his whole time wandering around listening to what's going on and if he's not doing that, he's looking out of the window up there on the first floor — he's at it now.'

Sarah turned round, following his pointed finger, and had the merest impression of a face before the lace curtain fell back into place.

'He's a right nutter, that bloke, if you ask me, and Kate thinks he's a peeping Tom. There's a large comprehensive school up the road and Kate says he's always there when the girls are walking past in the morning. Kate reckons they know exactly what he's up to; why else would they hitch their skirts so high, flash their knickers and wiggle their bums as they go past here? I'm sure that he's quite harmless, though. I gather that he did get a bit of grief after his old mother died — she used to look after him — but once the blokes in the pub found out about his quite remarkable memory, he became part of the furniture, so to speak. He became the star of the local quiz team and his odd behaviour is by and large accepted. Ask him who scored the most goals in the first division of the football league in 1934 and he'll come straight out with it and I've never known him to be wrong. If he enjoys watching the girls go by, so what, I say. A few months ago, I heard on the grapevine that some of the lads at the school were threatening to sort him out, but I and a few others aren't having any of that sort of thing round here and I had a quiet word with them. Anyway, if anyone knows what's happened to the person you're after, he will.'

'Thanks. Don't worry, we're not going to get the knuckle-dusters out. It's just a routine enquiry.'

The man grinned at her. 'I do shiftwork in security at the airport and I've heard that one before.'

For several minutes after Sinclair had first rung the bell and then banged on the door, Sarah thought that the man was not going to answer. She lifted the flap of the letterbox and was just about to give him a shout, when through the gap she saw him standing in the hall only a couple of feet away.

'Police,' she said. 'We're making enquiries about a young woman who used to live in the house across the road. I expect you saw me talking to the man who owns it now and he thought you might be able to help.'

Without replying, the man opened the door on its chain and inspected her warrant card through the gap.

'You'd better come in.'

The man standing in the dingy hall towered over Sarah and was a good three inches over Sinclair's six feet; as well as being tall, he was also very thin and almost bald, with several strands of grey-brown hair plastered across the top of his head. Despite the very warm day, he was wearing a sleeveless woollen sweater on top of his shirt and tie and his grey flannel trousers were held up by a brown leather belt.

'We're sorry to have disturbed you, but we're making enquiries about a young woman and her mother who used to live in the house opposite about four years ago. The present occupants only moved in about two years ago and don't know anything about her.'

'Yes, those people came here on 18 November 2005 — it was a Friday.'

'That's very impressive. How do you know that?'

'I'm good at remembering things.'

'Excellent, you're just the person we need,' Sinclair said. 'The mother and daughter are called Turner and perhaps this photograph of the young woman might help.'

The man took the print and examined it with great care, back and front.

'Yes, that is Rebecca Turner.'

'When did she leave here?'

'You'd better come into the front room.'

Although the room wasn't dirty, there was a musty air to it as if the windows hadn't been opened for months. The only items of furniture in it were a table and two chairs and a cheap sideboard with nothing on its top. On the wall above it was a poor reproduction of 'The Monarch of the Glen'.

The man cleared his throat. 'I'd better get another chair.'

Sinclair raised his eyebrows when the man had left and Sarah hastily wiped the grin off her face when he returned almost immediately, carrying a white-painted folding chair, which he opened out.

'What exactly do you want to know about her?' he said, when they were all sitting round the table.

'As much as you can remember.'

If Sarah had known what was to follow, she most certainly would not have put it like that. The man put the fingertips of both hands together and fixed his gaze somewhere over her left shoulder.

'The girl's mother came to the house opposite, number thirty-six on 16 January 1992, which was a Thursday, and she was pregnant at the time. My mother was still alive then and she remarked on it at once and went across straightaway with offers to help and a casserole she had just made.'

'And what was the woman's response?'

'She was extremely rude, saying she was able to manage very well on her own, thank you very much. My mother was most put out.'

'I presume she was still living there when the baby was born?'

'Yes, that took place in the local hospital on Tuesday 23 March 1993. It was a girl.'

Sarah tried not to show her astonishment and was relieved to see that the man was still not looking straight at her.

'You obviously know a lot about what goes on around here.'

'Yes, I do. The local Neighbourhood Watch committee relies on me a good deal.'

'I'm sure it does.'

It went on and on from there and a good forty-five minutes went by before they got up to leave. They discovered that the girl's mother never went out to work, doing some word processing at home, sending the results through the post. She never had any visitors and took part in none of the local activities. As for her daughter, she went to the local comprehensive school, which was only fifteen minutes walk away, but every day, come rain, come shine, she was invariably accompanied by her mother both there and back. The school had an excellent record in dealing with bullying on site, but it was a different story outside the grounds, which began in earnest when the girl reached adolescence. Rebecca Turner proved to be just the sort of girl to be meat and drink to the bullies; she was clever, but timid and unsure of herself. Even the presence of her mother failed to stop the shouting and jeering and there was even the throwing of the odd stone.

'How did Mrs Turner deal with that?' Sinclair asked.

'One of the hard men from the local estate started to take his pitbull for a walk each morning and afternoon along the same route and the kids soon got the message. You see, he was a dealer; some of the kids depended on him for their supplies and nasty things happened to people who got on the wrong side of him. That all stopped when he got nicked and he's still in prison. The estate's been much quieter since we saw the back of him.'

'From what you say, it sounds as if he was

protecting Rebecca and her mother, but how on earth would a woman like her manage to persuade him to do so, particularly as it appears from what you said that the two of them kept themselves to themselves?'

The man looked at them without any change of expression. 'There are ways apart from money, you know.'

'If you mean the sort of ways I imagine you mean, I would have thought that a man like that would have been able to find what he wanted elsewhere and, how shall I put it, in a more physically attractive and younger person.'

'Yes, but there aren't all that many people prepared to offer the services he required. You see, if one keeps one's eyes and ears open, one finds things out and he used to visit the house opposite once a week and it doesn't take forty-five minutes just to collect money, does it?'

'How long did that go on?'

'A little over a year. Would you like me to tell you the exact dates?'

'That won't be necessary. Why did it stop, do you suppose?'

'I told you, the bloke got nicked, didn't he? He got put away and for some reason, the kids continued to leave the girl alone after that.'

'What happened next?'

'The girl went away to work. She used to come back for weekends and sometimes for longer and then quite suddenly the mother moved away. There was one of those house clearances, the place was sold and no one knew where or why she had gone.'

Sinclair reached into the breast pocket of the jacket of his suit, took out his wallet and showed the man the photograph that Dr Cartwright had given them.

'Is that Mrs Turner?' The man nodded. 'We would be interested to know the exact date when she left.'

With scarcely a pause, the man told them the date, the day of the week and the precise time that the taxi had come.

When the two detectives left the house, they saw the young man opposite cleaning his car. He straightened up as they approached and grinned at them.

'How did you get on with our local oddball?'

'He was most helpful.'

'I thought he might be.'

'What an extraordinary man that was,' Sarah said when they were back in the car. 'How on earth did he manage to carry all those facts and times in his head? It's not as if he had any warning that we were coming.'

'I'm pretty sure he's a 'savant'. Have you heard of *Rain Man*?'

'Yes, I saw the film on TV some time ago.'

'Well, Raymond Babbitt, the man portrayed in it, is a real person. He has a remarkable memory for facts, but like many of those like him, he finds it difficult to relate to people and he has neurological deficits as well. Many others with these memory skills also have demonstrable brain abnormalities and some of them are autistic, but about half do not. It may sound an enviable skill, but forgetting is important for normal, well-integrated people and many psychologists believe that most if not all these savants have subtle brain dysfunction. Anyway, what that fellow told us puts the cat firmly amongst the pigeons.'

'It certainly does and clearly we need to pay the Turner/Crawford woman a visit, but we'll obviously have to check with Tyrrell first.'

'You're right. Why don't I drive and you can speak to him on your mobile?'

Tyrrell was in a meeting, but his secretary promised to get a message to him and to say that it was urgent. They were nearing the outskirts of London when he got through and he listened without comment as Sarah gave him the gist of what they had discovered.

'I see. Have you got the number of the place in Putney with you?'

'Yes, it's in my filofax.'

'Let me have it, then, and I'll see if she's in and fix a time for us to meet there. How long do you reckon it'll take you to get to Putney?'

'About an hour, I reckon.'

'Right. Unless there's any great urgency, it will probably have to be this evening as I'm tied up at the moment, but I'll ring you back in a few minutes to give you a time.'

He came back on the phone ten minutes later. 'Tyrrell here. Enid Crawford left that house some time on Monday morning, without, as far as the woman knows, taking anything with her and she hasn't been back since, nor left any message. I'd like you both to go straight there and let me know the score at home this evening unless you judge that it can't wait. I've told the woman to expect you within the next hour and a half.'

★   ★   ★

The late Victorian corner house in Putney was a few hundred yards north of the Upper Richmond Road and the outside had clearly been redecorated in the recent past, the black paintwork around the window frames and that of the front door being both unmarked

243

and smooth. The house was set back from the road with a semi-circular drive, the entrance and exit being separated by a bed filled with flowering shrubs. There was a wooden fence running along the pavement at right angles to the front of the property and this was interrupted by a garage door, which looked as if it hadn't been opened for years, a heavy-duty, very rusty padlock securing the stout bolt.

The woman who opened the door was dressed elegantly in a crisp white shirt and cashmere pullover, with tailored slacks.

'Ah, you must be the CID people,' she said crisply. 'I'm Celia Haddon. Come in.'

She showed them into the large sitting room immediately to the right of the front door, which was obviously used by the guests. There was a sofa, several easy chairs, a large television set sitting on a table and on the shelf below it a DVD player with a selection of discs by its side, a bookcase with a collection of paperback novels, detective stories and thrillers and a rack, resting on another table, containing leaflets with details of London attractions.

'I gather that Mrs Crawford went away some time last Monday morning,' Sinclair said.

'Yes. Mrs Walters, my cleaning lady, comes

in for a couple of hours every morning from 8.30 to 10.30 and as I wanted to choose some new lampshades at Peter Jones, I asked Mrs Crawford if she wouldn't mind holding the fort for me for a couple of hours or so after Mrs Walters had left. She's done that for me before. When I got back — it must have been a few minutes before one — and let myself in, there was no sign of her and there hasn't been since.'

'No note, no phone call?'

'No, nothing.'

'And I gather that, as far as you could see, she hadn't taken any of her belongings with her.'

'That's right.'

'Has she ever done that before? I mean, left without telling you?'

'Never.'

'What sort of a person is she?'

'Very quiet. More than that — withdrawn, I'd say. Whenever she was here, she never talked to the other guests and always used to get her own breakfast and took it up to her room before the others came down. A full cooked breakfast is on offer here, but she invariably stuck to cereal, some tinned fruit and toast and made her own coffee with the facilities that are provided in all the rooms. She had another peculiar habit, which was to make her own bed and clean both her room and bathroom. The first time she did it, I explained that that was all part of the service for which Professor Vaughan was paying, but she told me she preferred to do it herself and I have to admit that it was always immaculate when she left — a much higher standard, in fact, than Mrs Walters ever achieves.

'She's a strange woman, Mrs Crawford. She always answers if I speak to her, but I can't remember her ever having initiated a conversation.'

'How many guests do you take?'

'There are three single and two double rooms including the one that Enid Crawford used when Professor Vaughan had guests of her own. That was almost always at the weekend. The arrangement suited us very well; the professor always gave me plenty of notice and as nothing was ever sprung on us, it didn't interfere with the rest of our business.'

'What happened when the professor was on holiday?'

'Mrs Crawford stayed in the flat. I asked her once if she ever took a holiday herself and all I got in reply was a straight 'no'.'

'Do you manage this whole enterprise yourself?'

'No, my husband, who works in the City,

helps me by doing the accounts, the garden in the evening and at weekends and also bits and pieces of maintenance. You'd no doubt like to see Mrs Crawford's room.'

'Yes, please, we would.'

The room on the first floor would have been a good size had it not been for the bathroom, which had been partitioned off and contained a shower, basin and lavatory, but even so there was still room for the bed, chest of drawers, wardrobe and a small easy chair. Inevitably, too, there was a small TV set standing on a table.

'And has everything that she brought with her been left behind?' Sarah asked.

'Yes, as far as I am aware. Her nightdress is under the pillow and what clothes she had with her are in the chest of drawers and wardrobe, including her raincoat and umbrella. She brought them all from the flat in that holdall you can see on top of the wardrobe.'

'Was anyone else in the house apart from her when you left to go shopping?'

'No. Only two of the other rooms were taken the night before and both occupants departed soon after breakfast.'

At the woman's suggestion, they looked through all the rooms in the house, including the loft and cellar, but found nothing out of the ordinary.

'Did you ever meet Professor Vaughan?' Sinclair asked.

'Yes, when she first came to look at the room and discuss arrangements. One knew exactly where one was with her and I rather liked what little I saw of her. Terrible tragedy.'

'Yes, it is. How did she pay you?'

'Direct debit. She asked me to bill her separately for any extras, but there never were any.'

'Well, thank you very much. Would you let me know at once if Mrs Crawford turns up or contacts you in any way? I'll give you my mobile number.'

'Yes, of course.'

★   ★   ★

Sarah was sitting on the balcony at the rear of her flat and was just about to take a sip from the glass of white wine that Sinclair had poured out for her when her mobile phone rang and she raised her eyebrows and sighed deeply.

'No peace for the wicked. Hello . . . Yes, speaking . . . I see. I'll get some of our people over to you as soon as possible. In the meantime, please don't touch anything and make sure that no one goes near the garage. Are you all right yourself? . . . Good.

Inspector Sinclair and I will be with you in just a few minutes. Goodbye.'

'Mrs Haddon?'

'Yes. Her husband's just found the Crawford woman hanging from a rope in the garage.'

★ ★ ★

The two detectives arrived at the house in Putney only a few minutes before Tyrrell and were already talking to the owners in their private sitting room.

'I was just warning Mr and Mrs Haddon that the forensic team are on their way and that inevitably it is going to cause serious disruption to them,' Sarah said, after she had made the introductions. 'Rather than getting Mr Haddon to go over it twice, I suggested that we should wait until you got here before he described what he found.'

Tyrrell nodded and smiled at the couple. 'It must have been a great shock to you both and I would be most grateful if you would tell us exactly what happened.'

'Yes,' the powerfully built man, wearing a cotton shirt and slacks, said. 'It was still so hot when I got back from work that I decided to leave the lawn until this evening. I keep the mower in the old garage; it is completely detached from the house and access to it used to be in the side road, but it was in such a poor state of repair that we decided to use it for storage and garden equipment until such time as we had the funds to rebuild it. Luckily, there is also off-street parking in the drive at the front.

'Anyway, the rear door, which provides access from the garden, is badly warped, such that it won't shut properly and leaves a gap wide enough for me to get in, although I do have to give it a good shove to get the mower out. There was a light inside at one time, but the wiring was unsafe and I had it disconnected. Anyway, it took me a moment or two to adjust my eyes to the gloom and then I saw her. In my younger days, I was in the army and had a tour of duty in Northern Ireland, so I know a dead body when I see one, particularly if it has been undiscovered for some time in very hot weather, and so I decided to leave everything as it was and Celia rang your colleague.'

Tyrrell nodded. 'I'm very glad that you acted as you did — it makes our task a great deal easier. The forensic team should be here any minute and I doubt if they will need to disturb you for more than, say, a couple of hours; they will also need to have a careful look at the room you rented out to Professor

Vaughan. Mrs Haddon, I know that my two colleagues here spoke to you at some length about Mrs Crawford when they came here earlier today, but I wondered, if, in the light of her apparent suicide, you remember what her state of mind was like when you left her here earlier that day.'

The woman thought for a moment. 'I was going to say her usual withdrawn, dour and uncommunicative self, but now I come to look back in the light of what has happened, she seemed not exactly excited, but rather more animated and anxious than usual. I wouldn't want to make too much of it, but I do believe that she was worked up about something.'

'Do you know if she received any post or a phone call that morning?'

'Definitely not while I was here. I picked up the post myself and I would have noticed at once if there had been anything addressed to her. Not once in her many stays here did she receive so much as a card or a letter and I can only remember a few phone calls for her, all of which came from Professor Vaughan and the last one of those was many months ago.'

'Do you know if she had a mobile?'

'If she did I never saw it and there wasn't one when I looked through her belongings to see if I could find a contact address or phone number, when she disappeared.'

'I'm extremely sorry that you have been put to all this upset and trouble and we are extremely grateful to you for acting so swiftly and calmly. Would it be possible to open the garage door on the side street when forensic arrive? It would cause much less upset and disruption if they did so.'

Mr Haddon nodded. 'I know where the key to the padlock is, believe it or not, and no doubt one of your chaps would give me a hand if it's stuck.'

'Good, we'll wait for them outside and I'll mention it to one of them directly they arrive and get them to give you a shout when they're ready.'

Tyrrell led the way back down the drive and on to the pavement outside.

'Those Haddons are pretty cool customers, I must say; I can understand him, ex army and all that, but she seems every bit as calm and detached as he is.'

Pocock and his team arrived a few minutes later and Tyrrell had just shown them where to park outside the garage when a battered Citroën estate car came round the corner and, with a protesting squeak from its tired differential, turned into the drive in response to Tyrrell's wave.

'Oh God, I might have known, it's the toffs' brigade.'

Tyrrell wasn't in the least put out and the hint of a smile passed his lips as he saw Tredgold incongruously dressed in brown plus-twos and a matching cap.

'A marginally less agreeable sobriquet than 'Groucho', I would venture to suggest.'

The man let out a loud guffaw. 'Touché! You're lucky to have found me, if I may put it that way, as do I detect a hint of wellbred disapproval at the sight of my apparel? Even I have to indulge in a little recreation from time to time on a fine summer evening. They draw the line at mobiles on my course, even for me, can you believe it, but I have one of those vibrating devices, you see.' He suddenly turned towards Sarah. 'You've no need to look so shocked, young lady, I was not referring to that type of vibrating device. Anyway, luckily it didn't happen in the middle of my downswing or when I was taking on a tricky putt — and I was able to sneak behind a convenient oak tree after the thing went off. Well, what is it this time?'

'A woman by the name of Enid Crawford found hanging in the garage of this guest-house; she was Helen Vaughan's housekeeper.'

'Ah, the plot doth thicken, doth it not? Tell me more.'

Tyrrell explained about the arrangement that had been made for the woman when Helen Vaughan had had visitors and how she had seemingly disappeared three days earlier and had only been found when Mr Haddon had gone into the garage to get his mower.

'I see. Well, we'll be some time and I won't have anything for you today, or even tomorrow, and so I would suggest that we foregather in my office on Saturday morning at 8.30 sharp. Oh, and Brigadier, you'd better bring your troops with you.'

11

'This whole business is beginning to make rather more sense,' Tyrrell said to his two assistants when they had gathered in his office on the following morning. 'I have discovered that Professor Vaughan did indeed make a phone call from her personal line in her office at the hospital to her flat just after 7 p.m. on the Sunday evening when she was killed. It lasted no more than a couple of minutes, confirming what Mrs Crawford said. However, instead of merely requesting the details of the references she required, I suspect that Helen Vaughan must have asked the woman to bring a whole file, or at least a collection of papers, up to the hospital, giving her the pass numbers of the pad entry to the department. Maybe it was the opportunity she had been waiting for, or perhaps it was just a sudden impulse, but I suggest that she picked up the paperweight and smashed it against the professor's head.

'It seems to me clear from what those people you interviewed said that the Crawford woman was both obsessional and psychotic and that she blamed Helen

Vaughan for her daughter's suicide, which I suppose in an oblique way was true. The idea of killing Helen Vaughan, I suggest, had been with her ever since her daughter's death and making plans, insinuating herself into the professor's life and waiting for the right moment must have made the final reckoning all the sweeter. It's possible that on her way to the hospital she may not have had the intention of killing her there and then, but perhaps the sight of the paperweight led her to believe that she would never have a better opportunity. Any comments so far?'

'What you say makes good sense, sir,' Sinclair said, 'but would a psychotic person, as Enid Crawford obviously was, who had the presence of mind to remove the incriminating evidence of the paperweight and throw it into the Thames, or dispose of it in some other way, really have committed suicide when it must have seemed that she had got away with the murder?'

Tyrrell nodded. 'Sarah?'

'I agree with Mark. I can imagine a rational person being overcome with remorse at what he or she had done and committing suicide as a result, but we all know that Enid Crawford was not a rational person at all. The other interesting point is that she must have known exactly what happened at the appointments' committee that so clearly sparked off her hatred for Helen Vaughan, which surely must mean that her daughter rang her up directly afterwards to tell her all about it. And where does Professor McKenzie come into all this? Why did he support Rebecca Turner so strongly when it was obvious that she was nothing like as good as the other young woman who got the job?'

'Those are all good points,' Tyrrell said. 'Another interesting fact is that the only fingerprints found on the outside door handle and inside the office were those of Helen Vaughan and Miss Ashby, the professor's secretary. All that suggests that the Crawford woman was wearing gloves and that the whole thing was carefully thought out, but against that idea is that she could hardly have foreseen the phone call from Professor Vaughan. Perhaps the gloves were just a piece of good fortune from her point of view. I, too, have reservations about the suicide and one further piece of information that only came to light this morning makes them even stronger. You see, an outgoing call was made from the guesthouse on Monday morning after the owner had left on her shopping trip and the number called was that of the City Hospital. Not only that, it was put through to Professor McKenzie by his secretary and he was seen leaving by taxi soon after. I have arranged for him to meet us here to 'bring him up to date with our enquiries' and he should be here very soon.'

At that moment, the bell of his internal telephone rang.

'Tyrrell.'

'Professor McKenzie is here, sir.'

'Good. I'll send someone down for him.'

'Would you like me to go, sir?'

'Yes, Sarah, I would. I don't want him to think that this is too much of a production and as he hasn't seen you before, that would have some advantages.'

★ ★ ★

Tyrrell got to his feet as the man was shown in and shook him by the hand. 'Good of you to come. You've already met Detective Inspector Prescott and this is Detective Inspector Sinclair.'

McKenzie nodded at both of them and sat in the chair directly in front of Tyrrell's desk.

'Things very much came to a head two days ago,' Tyrrell said, looking at the man opposite him very directly. 'A woman, who was Helen Vaughan's housekeeper, was found hanging from a rope in the garage of the guesthouse where she had been staying following the murder of her employer. We have reason to believe that her death occurred some time last Monday morning and it was on that same morning that she made a telephone call to the hospital. It was to you, wasn't it, Professor McKenzie?'

There was a very long pause during which the man looked unblinkingly across the desk at Tyrrell. 'The time has clearly come for me to explain what happened right from the beginning.'

'I see. If you are quite sure, we need to go to an interview room with recording facilities and I recommend that you arrange for your solicitor to be present.'

The man nodded. 'There is no need for that.'

* * *

Alastair McKenzie was going through the rough draft of the paper he was due to give at a meeting of the Royal College of Pathologists when the telephone rang.

'McKenzie!'

'There's a lady on the line for you, sir. She said that she worked for you here a long time ago and felt sure you would wish to speak to her.'

'You'd better put her through.'

'Alastair, it's me.'

He knew at once who it was, recognizing the voice immediately, even though he hadn't heard it for all those years, and a shiver ran right down his spine.

'I'm in a house in Putney and I wish to see you. If you are not here by eleven, I will get in immediate touch with the police.'

He was given the address and before he had time to think of a reply, the woman had hung up. He took the A to Z out of a drawer in his desk and, finding the page, sat looking at it for a few moments. It would have to be a taxi and even if the traffic was reasonable, it was going to be a tight squeeze getting there in time.

In the preceding four years, he had tried and largely succeeded in putting it all out of his mind, but as he sat in the back of the cab, it all came back. Had it really been twenty-seven years since his life had fallen apart? The future had looked so bright. There he was at the age of thirty-five, already a consultant pathologist at a prestigious London teaching hospital, with the near certainty of becoming head of department and with a professorship likely to follow that within the next seven years. And then it happened. His wife, Mary, five years younger than him, already making a name for herself as a barrister and set to become a QC within a few years, had a devastating asthma attack while alone in her chambers and was left with such serious brain damage due to the lack of oxygen that right from the start he was told that there was no realistic hope of useful recovery. The doctors had been right; there she was all these years later, still in a nursing home, an empty husk of the vibrant person she had once been. Money was the least of his worries — her wealthy parents had set up a trust fund, which was large enough to allow her to be kept in comfort for the rest of her life. He was not to know that the rest of her life would be showing no signs of ending twenty-five years later.

He was to think that if he had let go right at the start, if he had given reign to his grief and despair, things might well have turned out very differently, but he didn't. Of course he didn't; it would have been against all his nature and upbringing. Whatever happened, however bad, one didn't give into it, one made the best of things and got on with one's life. That was the philosophy that had been dinned into him right from childhood and there was no way he would be able to change it.

If before it happened, he had been asked how he would have liked his colleagues to behave towards him if a tragedy had struck, he would undoubtedly have said that he did not want any fuss, just a few words of condolence and then to be left in peace. In the event, that's exactly what happened; it was as if they were embarrassed by him, which in fact was exactly what they were.

It was some three months after the tragedy had struck, when he was sitting in the living room of his flat one Saturday evening, looking sightlessly at the images on the television screen, that the bell rang and there was Anne Turner, carrying a bunch of flowers and a bottle of malt whisky.

His secretary, who had been with him for nearly a year, was quiet, efficient and reliable, but in no sense had he so much as glanced at her in the way that most healthy young men did at attractive women. The reason was obvious and that was that in no way did he find her attractive. It was not that she was ugly or even plain, just that she made no effort with her hair or clothes and her whole manner was forbidding.

'I'm sorry,' she said, her voice cracking. 'I'm so very sorry.'

After that it was a confused memory of comforting words, reassuring physical contact and finally a violent release of all his pent-up emotion and anger at the unfairness of it all.

He woke the following morning having slept properly for the first time since Mary, the only woman he had ever loved, had been taken from him. For a few minutes he lay there feeling relaxed and at peace, vaguely remembering the extraordinary dream that he had experienced. The realization that it had been no dream came to him slowly and then the evidence of the stains on the sheet, the flowers and the half-empty bottle of whisky on the table in the living room could no longer be denied.

He stood under the shower, the needle-sharp jets of cold water driving away any hope that it might all have been an illusion after all. Why had Anne done it? How was he going to be able to face her at the hospital? In the event, he didn't have to; on his desk, when he went into work that morning, was her letter of resignation, with a copy to the personnel manager, stating that her mother had been disabled by a stroke that weekend, that she now had to look after her full-time and apologizing for the lack of notice.

The practicalities of her sudden departure were soon dealt with by the hospital administrators and first a temporary replacement and then a permanent secretary were appointed. That was the easy part, but what if anything was he to do about Anne? He couldn't just leave it like that, or could he? He had never had the slightest inclination towards her in that way and, in all honesty, he could say that the same was true of any other woman once he had married Mary. Anne had come to him when he was at his most vulnerable and on top of that he had drunk so much that he couldn't even remember how they had got into the bedroom, let alone what had followed. Why had she behaved in the way she did? Even though he was naïve in the extreme where the opposite sex was concerned, every conceivable idea went through his mind, each one seemingly more ridiculous than the preceding one. Could she even have had a secret longing for him and got carried away, wanting to help him in the only way she was able to in his obvious sadness and depression? The very idea was ridiculous; had he been asked, which of course he hadn't, he would have said that like Miss Buss and Miss Beale, she was not the sort of person ever to have felt Cupid's darts.

It was some five months later that once again she came back into his life. When he opened the door in answer to the ring, without saying anything she lifted up her skirt, lowered her panties a few inches and revealed the all too obvious pregnancy. In exactly the same way as she had done when she was his secretary, everything was explained and then confirmed on a sheet of paper in her accurate and error-free typing. In order to ensure her silence, her maintenance and that of the child were to be continued until full-time education was over. The amount with inflation linking was to be paid by direct debit on a monthly basis. Failure to comply would result in disclosure to his wife's parents, the authorities at the hospital and university, his colleagues in the pathology department and maybe the General Medical Council and the press would be interested, too. For her part, she promised to keep him in touch with his daughter's progress — she already knew that the foetus was a girl. There was to be no discussion and the first payment was to be made within the following two weeks. With that, she walked straight out of his flat.

How was he going to handle the situation? He thought about blood tests, but he was O positive himself, the most common group, and how was he to get a blood sample as she clearly had no intention of letting him near the child after it was born? Every other alternative went through his mind — to his shame he even very briefly considered killing her, but in the event, he did just as he had been ordered. After all, he had modest tastes and the amount of money demanded was well within his compass.

He had to admit that Anne Turner kept her side of the bargain, writing to him each year on the girl's birthday, charting her progress at school and never demanding more money than they had agreed. It was soon after the girl's eighteenth birthday that a longer letter arrived, for the first time including an address and setting out her predicted A level results and indicating that she expected him to get her into the City Hospital Medical School. 'I have kept track of your career and now that you are dean,' the letter went on, 'that should not be too much to ask of you.'

It had been quite subtly done and although there were no direct threats, there were nevertheless hints that the future might well not be so smooth if he didn't comply.

The girl, whom he saw for the first time when she attended the admissions' interview, looked very like her mother and he saw immediately that he was going to have his work cut out to get her accepted, even though the other two members of the panel were considerably junior to him and would be unlikely to go against his opinions.

By that time, McKenzie had had a great deal of experience in selecting students and in normal circumstances, although he would have listened carefully to what she had to say and treated her courteously as he did every candidate, he would have rejected her almost straightaway. If he had not read her references beforehand, he would have been able to predict them within minutes of starting to talk to her. Excelling at coursework, dedicated to her other studies, excellent grades predicted, would make an outstanding doctor were what he would have expected and that is exactly what he got from her school. What he saw, though, was a diffident, anxious young woman, desperately keen to please and with no experience of the outside world. Where was the independence of thought and action he looked for in candidates, the imaginative gap year, the Duke of Edinburgh awards, the outside interests?

He felt desperately ashamed that he had engineered her acceptance ahead of better candidates. Despite his position as dean, he realized that he would never have got his way had he not been chairman of the panel and that the other members were a recently appointed consultant, who was anxious to please and the other who was shamelessly biased in favour of her own sex. McKenzie, as he knew perfectly well himself, had a reputation for having reservations about women working in the front-line specialities in hospital medicine, not least because of the expense and logistical complications engendered by time off for pregnancies and domestic crises. It was all very well for people to say that times had changed and that women in medicine were now in the ascendancy and that with flexible working practices, it was perfectly possible to deal with those eventualities, but where was the continuity? And what about having to accept that after taking off six months after childbirth, or even the year that was already being talked about, surgeons needed to be eased back into work, even retrained like airline pilots, not to mention the difficulty of finding locums and their expense.

In the event, the male on the panel being anxious to please the dean and the woman gratified at his seeming conversion to her cause, Rebecca Turner was given a place at the medical school and did manage to qualify with only a few minor hiccups on the way. McKenzie kept an eye on her progress and when she left to do her house jobs — she hadn't proved anything like impressive enough to have obtained one at the City — he was convinced that the nightmare was over at last. What had his feelings been towards the young woman? In one way he felt completely detached from her and yet, in another, disappointed that a daughter of his should have had such a flat personality, lacking any sparkle or social charisma. On the occasions, too, when he watched her with the other students, he sensed that the other females found her boring and, as for the males, they never so much as glanced at her with any hint that they might have found her sexually attractive.

Immediately she had qualified, he wrote to Anne Turner saying how pleased he was that Rebecca had done so well and stopped his regular payments. In return, the woman sent him a book that charted his daughter's life from her birth until her qualification. It was done in obsessional detail, with charts of her physical growth, her first tooth preserved in a tiny envelope, a lock of her hair, school reports, photographs on each birthday and on seaside holidays, with records of her school career and visits to pantomimes, circuses and films.

His peace of mind was shattered eighteen months later when almost simultaneously he saw that Rebecca was one of the candidates for the senior house office post in Helen Vaughan's section of haematology in his department and he received another letter from Anne Turner, telling him that she expected Rebecca to get the job. Somehow the lack of any specific threat in it made it even more chilling.

McKenzie knew immediately that this time he wasn't going to succeed. It proved difficult enough to get her shortlisted and the idea that Helen Vaughan would accept her against the two really good candidates, one of whom, as it happened, was another female, was absurd.

He did his best, but the inevitable had happened and after the young woman's tragic suicide that very evening, he fully expected Anne Turner to expose him, or to make other demands. In his mind's eye, he could see the headlines in the tabloids, photographs of Rebecca and himself, his disgrace and forced resignation. When none of that happened and time went by, he really did believe that it was all over, but then Helen Vaughan was murdered and that was followed, a week later, by the phone call. When Anne ordered him to go over to Putney, he did hesitate, but only for a moment, knowing that if he didn't confront her now, the nightmare would go on pursuing him for the rest of his life.

If he had passed her in the street, he would never have recognized the woman who opened the door of the house in Putney, even though her appearance as she had been all those years ago was etched in his memory.

She had aged badly and had lost a lot of weight and with her thinning grey hair and lined face, she looked a good ten years older than the early fifties he knew her to be.

Without saying a word, she made a gesture towards the door off the hall to her right and pointed to one of the chairs by the side of the table.

'Sit down, Alastair.'

He did so carefully and precisely. He undid the button on his jacket and looked across at her unblinkingly, while she took the seat opposite him and tried to stare him down. After perhaps thirty seconds, for the first time he saw uncertainty in her expression and she was the first to lower her gaze.

'Rebecca,' she said, after a long pause, 'rang me up directly she had been turned down for that post in your department and told me exactly what had happened. She was utterly distraught and that woman Helen Vaughan killed her as surely as if she had cut her throat. Rebecca also told me that you had been nice to her when she was interviewed for her entry to the medical school and at the appointments' committee, but being nice wasn't enough for our daughter, was it, Alastair, not nearly enough? You bear almost as much responsibility for her death as that woman and deserve the same fate, although that would be too merciful. You are going to regret what you did and failed to do for the rest of your life — I am going to see to that.

'I can see that you realize now that I was Rebecca's avenger. I am a very patient person, Alastair, and the four years it took to plan, get close to that woman and finally achieve revenge for what she did only added to the satisfaction when the time finally came. I will never forget the sound of that paperweight landing on the side of her head, crushing her skull as easily as if it had been an eggshell. The only pity is that she didn't suffer the mental pain that I have had to endure.

'She played into my hands, you see. I told the police that I was rung up by Helen Vaughan that evening as she wanted a reference from one of the files in her flat, which she had forgotten to take with her. She did ring me up all right and I knew that the call would be logged by the telephone company, but she didn't require just a reference, she wanted a complete file and asked me to take it to the hospital and gave me the code for entry into the pathology department.

'I hadn't set out with the intention of killing her then, but the paperweight was truly a gift from God. The very moment that

I saw it, I knew that it had been placed right in front of me for the very purpose I put it to. I wasn't so excited, either, that I became careless. It was pure good fortune that I should have been wearing gloves so I had no need to worry about fingerprints or the fashionable DNA. I knew all about that, of course. How could I not with all the typing I had done for that woman? I took the paperweight with me; dropped it into a skip that I came across in the road outside a house on my way back to the underground station. The entrance hall was deserted and the tissues and gloves went into a litter bin there.

'As for you, Alastair, I'm going to see . . . '

McKenzie, who had been looking intently at her across the table, suddenly held up his hand and she suddenly stopped in mid-sentence.

'You keep referring to Rebecca as our daughter and that was what I believed until you took that last step of ordering me to get her a job in my department. You see, I realized then that I had been wrong in thinking that it was all over and from that moment I knew it was never going to be. It was then that I remembered that book that you sent me. DNA testing of many different samples wasn't available when all this started, but it is now, as you are aware, and it is perhaps poetic justice that Helen Vaughan should have been one of those who made it possible. You see, there was a tooth and a lock of Rebecca's hair in that book you sent me and I had both of them tested as well as a sample from myself. I even went as far as to confirm it by a specimen from the autopsy after the girl's tragic suicide. The attendant at that forensic laboratory used to work for me at one time and it was easy to find an excuse for asking him to give me another sample.

'You were already pregnant when you came to my flat to offer your sympathy when I was at my lowest ebb, weren't you? You have no need to answer. I know you were. Why didn't I realize it or suspect it earlier? Partly, I think, it was because I wasn't thinking straight at the time and I was also incredibly naïve where sexual matters were concerned, both unworldly and inexperienced.

'As well as being a murderess, you were also the one who was responsible for Rebecca's suicide. You pushed her obsessively way beyond her capabilities; all right, she was intelligent enough, but she wasn't psychologically robust enough, nor did she have the right personality for a career in medicine.'

'So you got there in the end, but it took you long enough, didn't it, Alastair?' the

274

woman said with a sneer. 'And what does the great professor think he is going to do about it?'

'As a start, I hardly think that the police won't be interested in what you've been saying. You appear to have forgotten already that you have admitted to me that you murdered Helen Vaughan.'

'Do you really think that they'll believe you if you say that? If you do, you're a bigger fool than I took you for and I should know. Helen Vaughan wasn't quite so discreet as no doubt you fondly imagined. You see, she took me for a nonentity and from time to time, when we were taking a coffee break during long dictation sessions, she would let slip a few indiscretions, not, of course, without a few subtle promptings from the grey and uninteresting woman by her side. Helen Vaughan didn't like you much, Alastair, and more than that, thought you were not a good head of department, not a real scientist and that you had no time for women in medicine. She also knew that you didn't like the idea of her succeeding you and would do your utmost to see that it didn't happen. Your reputation, of which I gather you are so proud, wouldn't survive a few revelations like that, would it, Alastair, even if Helen Vaughan's murder wasn't pinned firmly on you? People would have their suspicions, wouldn't they?'

McKenzie suddenly stood up and gave the heavy table a push away from him, holding on to it and trapping the woman sitting opposite him against its side.

'You may have been an efficient secretary at one time, but that was more than twenty years ago and you probably don't realize just how advanced these pocket recorders have become. A fool I may be, but not such a one as to come here totally unarmed.'

He pulled the machine out of the pocket of his jacket, held it up for a moment, flicked the switch on it, then strode out of the room and the house without looking back. Nor did he do so as he went round the corner to the taxi, which was waiting for him.

*　*　*

'Do you have the recorder with you?'

'Yes, but unfortunately it won't be of any use,' McKenzie said. He reached into his pocket and handed it across the desk. 'You see, I was bluffing; I did have it with me, but I never switched it on and in any case, it might well not have picked up her voice from inside my jacket. Indeed, the idea only came to me as I was speaking to her right at the end and it suddenly occurred to me that her believing that her confession had been recorded might free me from her at last.'

'Did you at any time consider that she might commit suicide?'

'Frankly, when I heard about it, I could hardly believe it and still find it difficult to do so. She was angry, certainly, but on thinking about my meeting with her, and I have done almost nothing else since it happened, it never occurred to me that she might be about to kill herself, but who knows what goes through people's minds in situations like that? No doubt she felt that I had been partly responsible for Rebecca's death and that hounding me for the rest of her life would be my sentence. Then, when she suddenly realized that she had confessed to Helen's murder and that it had been recorded, perhaps she did it on a sudden impulse. Who knows? I certainly don't.'

Tyrrell nodded in Mark Sinclair's direction, who signed off, giving the time and date, and then switched off the recording machine.

'Thank you for being so frank, Professor,' Tyrrell said. 'The stenographer will transcribe it all for you and I would like you to read it through very carefully and then sign it. I may need to see you again and if so, I will get in touch with you.'

'Will I have to give evidence at the inquest?'

'That will be up to the coroner.'

12

Eric Tredgold looked up from the report he was reading and let out a long-suffering sigh as he saw his secretary standing at the door.

'Am I not to be allowed the merest hint of peace and quiet, Miss Tombs? What is it this time?'

'It's Superintendent Tyrrell and his team, sir. I left a note on your desk last night to remind you that they were coming.'

'Reminders,' he barked, 'I don't need reminders. Show 'em in, woman, and while you're at it, you'd better get down to that furniture store round the corner and replace the chair that that obese colleague of mine, Hilton, destroyed the other day. We're going to need another one, unless you're expecting that nice plump young woman to sit on my lap.'

'I think we can cope without her having to do that, sir. Inspector Sinclair has offered to move the spare one in my office.'

Tredgold raised his eyebrows. 'Has he, has he indeed? Well, tell him to get on with it, then.'

The pathologist remained seated as the detectives filed in, peering intently at them over the top of his half-moon spectacles.

'If this goes on much longer, Miss Tombs,' he said in his rasping voice, as he watched the three detectives file in, 'I'll have to take out a hefty loan. Surely we must be scraping the bottom of the exchequer with such extravagant hospitality.'

'I think we'll just about be able to manage, sir, but if we are to stay above water, it will mean cutting back on such expensive biscuits.'

The man looked up at the ceiling and let out a long sigh. 'Enough of my travails, my dear Tyrrell, good morning to you and you, my dear. A little feminine pulchritude is just what's needed to brighten my flagging spirits. I must say I wasn't expecting a furniture removal man as well, but you're very welcome, too, my good fellow.'

Sinclair gave a little bow and put the chair down with elaborate care, dusted it with his handkerchief and offered it to Sarah.

'Thank you,' she said, smiling at both Sinclair and the man behind the desk.

'Well, my dear Tyrrell,' the pathologist said, 'the pleasantries being over, why not tell me what new gems of information you have for my delectation?'

Tyrrell opened his briefcase and lifted out several sheets of paper. 'I have here a transcript of the interview we had with Professor McKenzie yesterday and this copy is for you to study at your leisure. However, for the purposes of our discussion I will do my best to give you a summary.'

He explained how Anne Turner had tricked McKenzie into believing that he was the father of her child and how she was obsessed with her daughter, grooming her for a career in medicine, and how she pressured the man into getting her into the City Medical School. However, when it all went wrong and the young woman failed to get the haematology job at the hospital she had set her heart on and committed suicide, the woman's obsessions became centred on getting revenge on the two people she blamed for her daughter's death.

'Helen Vaughan and Alastair McKenzie, no doubt.'

'Precisely. It took her four years to develop and carry out her plan and after she had succeeded in killing Helen Vaughan by hitting her with that paperweight, she rang McKenzie at the hospital some days later, persuaded him to go to the house in Putney and taunted him with her account of what she had done and how she was now proposing to wreck his career and standing in the community. He happened to have his dictating machine in his pocket and although it wasn't switched on, he managed to convince her that he had recorded her rantings and that the police were certain to be interested in them. Then he claims to have walked out, having prevented her from following him by pushing the table against her and the chair in which she was sitting.'

'And no doubt, you're wondering if our friend Alastair was telling porkies and in fact gave her a helping hand by putting her head in the noose, having lost his cool.' Tredgold gave Sarah one of his vulpine smiles. 'I trust, young lady, that you appreciate my use of contemporary syntax.'

'Yes, sir, I'm most impressed by your facility with it.'

'Good. That's more than can be said of Miss Tombs. She was quite upset when I said that someone who had suffered an unpleasant sexual assault must have been taken aback. No sense of humour, that woman. Where was I? Oh yes, the question of whether this Crawford/Turner woman hanged herself or suffered an assisted death. What is the view of your team, Tyrrell?'

'I'd prefer it if they spoke for themselves. All three of us have contributed to the investigation and not surprisingly have slightly different slants on it. Perhaps DI

Prescott might set the ball rolling?'

Tredgold nodded. 'An admirable idea, my dear Tyrrell,' he said, looking towards Sarah and raising his eyebrows. 'We know each other of old, don't we, my dear, and I can't see you being taken aback by anything I say.'

Sarah had a sudden vision of what she and Mark had been doing in the boat on the river and concentrated all her attention on what she was about to say, willing herself not to look away or blush.

'I can't pretend to know a great deal about mental illness,' she said, 'but if a mother invests her whole life in a child from before birth until adulthood and then sees everything snatched away from her in such a devastating way as by the girl's suicide, I don't find it that surprising that she should then go after the people she considered responsible, killing one of them and seeking to destroy the other. Then, if she suddenly realized that she had been found out and tricked into confessing what she had done, I don't find it surprising, either, that she should have killed herself.'

'Sinclair?'

'I think Sarah put it with admirable clarity. I agree entirely with her assessment of the woman, that is, until her death. Would someone as driven and fixated as she obviously was have taken that way out? I wonder. The only other possibility seems to me to be that McKenzie killed her. He is a powerful man. It is no exaggeration to say that his life has in many ways been blighted, firstly by the appalling tragedy that befell his wife and then what followed with Anne Turner. Did he finally crack, strangle her, then string her up in the garage? I think it unlikely but definitely a possibility.'

The pathologist nodded again. 'And how about you, Tyrrell, what is your reaction to these admirably articulate associates of yours?'

'Well,' the detective replied, 'we are all agreed that Anne Turner murdered Helen Vaughan and why she did so, but I'm concerned about McKenzie's story of the recorder in his pocket. Firstly, if he had planned what he was going to do in advance, he most certainly wouldn't have failed to turn it on; on the other, if it had been there by chance, would he have suddenly had the idea of bluffing her, taking into account the stress he must have been under at the time? On the other hand, would he have been able to fake her suicide so cleverly? He would presumably have had to strangle her in that room, carry her out into the garage and then set up what he hoped would make it look as if she had committed suicide. We are obviously dependent on your findings, Eric, but would McKenzie have been able to have done all of it with sufficient skill to deceive an experienced forensic pathologist? I don't think so.

'Most of what McKenzie said fits in with what my assistants — who, incidentally, did most of the work — discovered about Anne Turner and you must also have read our reports. She was obviously totally obsessed by her daughter and the need to make her into a successful doctor and when it went wrong and the young woman killed herself, her obsessions became centred on the two people whom she considered responsible for it. Her actions throughout only make sense in the context of her being mad. It would need a psychiatrist to put a label on the condition and a gloss on the reasons, but I personally take the view that frequently there is no explanation for such behaviour other than that these people are mentally deranged — obsessive psychopaths, if you like — and whether that is due to faulty development, acquired brain damage or upbringing is by the way. We have seen how Helen Vaughan, her mother and her daughter, Emily, in their different ways, all eventually managed to cope successfully with the severe emotional trauma they all suffered and, in my experience, this is very often the case with people with basically robust personalities.

'Anyway, I don't think there can be any reasonable doubt about Anne Turner having killed Helen Vaughan, but like the rest of my team, I have had some reservations about the woman having committed suicide. However, we need the benefit of your expertise and the findings of the scene-of-crime team to settle the matter, if indeed that is possible.'

'I must say it is a relief to find everything summarized so clearly and, what's more, in English. Correct grammar, clear articulation, no glottal stops and no crippling ers and ums; it is enough to make those of us who decry the adverb-deficient multitude 'scarce forbear to cheer', while the aforementioned illiterates would no doubt nod their heads and cry: 'the boys and girl done good.'

'Enough of that, I hear you cry,' Tredgold said, looking at all of them in turn, 'no doubt you wish to hear my final conclusions on this sorry affair. Well, if McKenzie did kill her, as you pointed out, my dear Tyrrell, he would have had to render her unconscious in the dining room, carry her out to the garage, string her up after leaving her handprints on the back of the chair, which was found lying

286

on its side. He would also have had to put some of the dust from the seat of that chair on the soles of her shoes, all without bruising her body at all. She was certainly alive for some time after the chair was removed from under her feet, presumably by her kicking it away. There were ante-mortem bruises around her neck as well as abrasions, no doubt caused by her jerking about, and she may even have had second thoughts as there was damage to a couple of her nails and some blood on the rope as she perhaps tried to loosen it. Apart from her neck and fingers, there were no other injuries to her body and no signs of any other form of violence.

'From all that regrettable verbosity, you will no doubt long since have gathered that the evidence for suicide is as near conclusive as evidence of that sort ever is.'

Tyrrell nodded. 'Thank you. We will have to trace the taxi driver who transported McKenzie from and back to the hospital and get forensic to look at his clothes and shoes, but in view of what you've said I don't expect them to find anything of interest. Oh, and one last thing; you probably noted that the woman admitted to having used the paper-weight as a weapon. She claims to have disposed of it in a skip on her way back to Wimbledon and I suppose we'd better at least

We do hope that you have enjoyed reading this large print book.

Did you know that all of our titles are available for purchase?

We publish a wide range of high quality large print books including:
Romances, Mysteries, Classics
General Fiction
Non Fiction and Westerns

Special interest titles available in large print are:
The Little Oxford Dictionary
Music Book
Song Book
Hymn Book
Service Book

Also available from us courtesy of Oxford University Press:
Young Readers' Dictionary
(large print edition)
Young Readers' Thesaurus
(large print edition)

For further information or a free brochure, please contact us at:
Ulverscroft Large Print Books Ltd.,
The Green, Bradgate Road, Anstey,
Leicester, LE7 7FU, England.
Tel: (00 44) 0116 236 4325
Fax: (00 44) 0116 234 0205

DESERVING DEATH

Peter Conway

Sixteen-year-old Sophie Hammond's parents are desperately worried by her moods and withdrawn behaviour. Fearing that she might be taking drugs, they send Sophie as a boarder to Sandford College, a private school. When she's found dead in her room, it's assumed that she has either taken her own life, or accidentally overdosed on drugs. However Rawlings, the forensic pathologist, is convinced that she has been suffocated. Then there are two further deaths . . . The lives of all those involved, including the investigating police officers, are turned upside down before the answers to the tragedy are found.